40 and Flirting (with Disaster)

SILVER FOXES OF BLACK WOLF'S BLUFF
BOOK FIVE

ELLA SHERIDAN

Blurb

He's the town's most eligible bachelor, which makes him completely off limits to the town's most recent—and reluctant—bachelorette.

Iris Daniels thought her life was set—twenty-plus years of marriage, two adult children, and a job she loves as Black Wolf's Bluff's librarian. Until her husband drops a bomb that destroys her complacency. Six months post-divorce isn't long enough to fully heal, so why is the pull of Gatlinburg's most eligible bachelor—and the man who knows her darkest secret —so strong?

Jamie Worthington accidentally overheard Kirk Daniels's outrageous proposal for his now ex-wife. That moment changed Iris's life forever—and gave Jamie the opening he never thought he would have. He's determined to show Iris that she's still a "sexy librarian," no matter her age, and that he wants her for his own, even if she thinks being with him is a recipe for disaster.

Praise for Silver Foxes of Black Wolf's Bluff

"[A] fascinating series."

"Fun, easy to read, and the start of what seems to be a dynamite series."

"Loved the town and omg that passion between JD and Lily burned the pages!!! Amazing book!"

"Where sexual tension and drama really heats up in the kitchen."

"Going back to Black Wolf's Bluff … was such a delight."

Also by Ella Sheridan

Silver Foxes of Black Wolf's Bluff

40 and (Tired of) Faking It

40 and (No Longer) Fighting It

40 and (Finally) Fixing It

40 and Flashing (the Scotsman)

40 and Flirting (with Disaster)

Assassins

Assassin's Mark

Assassin's Prey

Assassin's Heart

Assassin's Game

Southern Nights

Teach Me

Trust Me

Take Me

Southern Nights: Enigma

Come for Me

Deceive Me

Destroy Me

Deny Me

Desire Me

Archai Warriors

Griffin Undone

Phoenix Falling

If Only

Only for the Weekend

Only for the Night

Only for the Moment

Only If You Stay

Secrets

Unavailable

Undisclosed

Unshakable

For news on Ella's new releases, free book opportunities, and more, sign up for her VIP Reader List at ellasheridanauthor. com .

Join Ella's Escape Room on Facebook for daily fun, games, and first dibs on all the news!

Silver Foxes of Black Wolf's Bluff: 40 and Flirting (with Disaster)

Copyright © 2025 Ella Sheridan

Cover Design: Sweet 'n' Spicy Designs

Photographer: Jeanne Woodfin

Cover Model: Sean Ray

Published in the United States

One

Walking a tightrope sucked. Seriously sucked. Big fat donkey balls, as some of the teenagers who came into the library would say. Too bad Iris found herself doing it more and more lately.

Because of the man across the table from her. The one who refused to look up from his phone.

"Your steak, ma'am."

She startled at the waiter's words. Plastering a smile on her face, she glanced up at the young man. "Thank you."

Kirk grunted as he pocketed his cell—finally—the sound filled with displeasure. What had she done now?

Her husband glowered as the waiter set a full plate in front of him as well. Without a word of thanks, he dug in. Iris graced the waiter with another smile, this one apologetic. He returned it with a friendly nod that told her he didn't blame her for Kirk's lousy attitude.

If only it were that easy.

She picked up her knife and fork. "Happy anniversary, Kirk."

Twenty-three years. They'd spent twenty-three years together—as partners, lovers, parents. How was it that she felt less and less like she knew him as the years wore on? A stranger sat in the fancy leather-and-oak dining chair across from her, so closed-off and silent she was hard-pressed to say she actually knew him at all. And yet the way he held his polished silver fork, the way he chewed, the way he sipped from the cut-crystal wineglass were all intimately familiar.

How had it come to this?

Kirk's plate was clean, hers barely touched when he finally spoke. He wiped his mouth with a snowy-white linen napkin, then settled his fisted palms against the table. "This is no longer working for me, Iris."

Iris's gaze leaped to meet Kirk's. Her heart jumped into her throat, yet her face felt frozen. Carefully placing her silverware atop her china plate, she pushed it to the side. Shame filled her at her initial reaction: *he wants a divorce,* followed by a strong surge of relief. Maybe that had been the withdrawal she'd sensed the past few months. "'This'?"

"Us."

This is it. This is really it.

What am I going to do?

First, *speak.* "You want to divorce?"

His glare had her jerking back in her seat. Actual fear thumped in the pulse at her throat. "Hell no, I don't want a divorce."

She ignored the cursing. "Then what are you talking about?"

He had the grace to glance around, checking that they had no audience. Little late for that. But the Carousel had seated them at a table atop a dais in honor of the special occasion, slightly separated from the rest of the dining room. "I'm talking about you, Iris." He waved a hand in her direction. "You're not the woman I married anymore."

She scoffed. "I hope to God not, just like you're not the same. It's been twenty-three years, Kirk."

His mouth tightened, his eyes narrowing. "You're doing

2

things I don't like, things *my wife* shouldn't do. Voting against me at the city council meetings. Going dancing at the bar with your friends—without me. Showing yourself off to other men—"

She cut him off. "I'll vote however I feel led to vote. I don't need your permission, husband or not. And I didn't go to a bar; I went to the local pub. You were perfectly welcome to come along." But he'd refused, just as he'd refused most of her invitations to do things together recently. She'd been surprised he'd made reservations for their anniversary, frankly. But maybe he'd had this planned all along. As to the *showing herself off to other men*... "Is this about that Halloween costume again? Kirk, it was fine. Everything was covered."

"You appeared in town as a saloon girl, Iris," he hissed. "Every man who walked by got a clear idea of what is supposed to be mine."

She and her friend Scarlett had dressed up in the old-fashioned can-can girl costumes to run the photo booth at the Halloween carnival a few weeks ago. The flirty skirt had called to her, complete with crinoline and fishnet stockings, but she hadn't shown anything more than would be visible had she worn a fitted blouse and full skirt to work.

The stubborn look on her husband's face told her she wasn't going to win this argument—again. Still she couldn't hold back her, "That's ridiculous."

Kirk's glare narrowed on her. "It was the last straw. And frankly, I don't want what every other man has seen."

If he'd slapped her across the face, she couldn't have been more shocked. Her brain tried frantically to make sense of the whole conversation. "So you don't want me," she said, her lips feeling numb. "But you don't want to divorce."

"What I want is an open marriage."

In the stunned silence that followed his words, she became aware of a solid presence mere feet from their table. Raising her eyes, she caught sight of crisp black dress pants, masculine hands cupping a delicate china dessert plate, a fresh white dress shirt, and, finally, startled green eyes staring right into hers.

What I want is an open marriage rang in her ears, and as she stared into the man's eyes, she knew from the fixed expression on his face that he'd heard the same words she had.

The man cleared his throat. "We at the Carousel wanted to wish you a happy anniversary." He settled the cake, its single silver candle flickering with bright flame, at the edge of their table, equidistant between her and Kirk. "If you have need of anything"—somehow that stare made her feel like the words were meant for her—"please don't hesitate to ask."

The man excused himself, and the silence at the table became deafening. Iris fisted her shaking hands and forced herself to speak.

"So you want us to see other people but stay married."

"No." Kirk balled up his napkin and threw it onto his empty plate. "*I* want to see other people but stay married."

She couldn't help the laugh that escaped. "I dressed like a 'floozy'"—she made air quotes—"so you don't want me, but you do want to find someone else to sleep with?"

"A man has needs, Iris."

"So do women. And if you don't intend to fulfill those needs, I will definitely be looking elsewhere." She didn't want to, had no intention of doing any such thing, but what was good for the goose…

Kirk leaned across the table, his anger forcing her back in her seat. "You're not gonna play the whore on me, damn it."

"No." She balled up her own napkin, resolve firming inside her despite the shaking of her hands. She threw the napkin onto her plate just as he had, then leaned over to blow out the candle on their anniversary cake. "I won't be playing the whore on you. I won't be married to you anymore." Standing, she grasped her purse, facing Kirk squarely. "I will not live with a man who could even think about suggesting such a thing to me. I deserve more." So much more. "We're getting a divorce."

As she brushed by his chair, Kirk gripped her wrist tightly. "Iris—"

"Anything I can do for you, ma'am?"

The deep voice belonged to the man who had delivered the cake. Iris had hoped to avoid the humiliation of seeing him again, but right now she had no choice. She forced herself to meet those deep green eyes. "Yes. A cab, please."

The man nodded but refused to move, his gaze locking on Kirk's fingers tight around her arm. Glancing down, she realized that later she'd have bruises, though no pain registered right now.

She turned back to her husband of twenty-three years. They wouldn't make it to twenty-four. "I hope you already have her picked out, Kirk."

His hold tightened until his knuckles turned white. "Who?"

"The woman you want to sleep with." Because it was a sure bet he hadn't taken this risk without someone already in mind. "You can start tonight. Don't bother coming home."

Yanking her wrist from his grip, she turned and followed the man who'd interrupted them, ignoring Kirk as he called her name behind her. She refused to cry, not here. At home, when she was alone, she could let go.

Alone. That word opened up a vision of her future that she'd never expected to see. A solitary future. And shameful or not, the relief from earlier returned to mix with the pain clenching her stomach into a knot.

Alone. It sounded better than what Kirk had proposed.

The room was a blur of color and sound as they passed through. Iris kept her focus on the broad back of the man escorting her, ignoring everything else. He had placed a cell phone to his ear, she assumed to call her a ride as she'd requested. Her glance took in the red curls brushing his collar, sprinkled liberally with salt and pepper, the wide shoulders that looked like they could handle any burden. There was something familiar about him, something she couldn't place with her mind in chaos. She couldn't see his left hand to look for a ring, but she bet he'd never tell his wife he wanted to fool around on her. Or maybe he would. She'd never thought her ultra-conservative husband would suggest such a thing. He'd never wanted anything wild in the bedroom; they'd never even had anal sex.

Would he do that with his bimbo? He had made it plain she was the problem, not lack of desire for sex. What if—

She hadn't realized the man had stopped in front of her until she slammed into his side. As if he'd anticipated her distraction, he'd turned, and neatly caught her with a light hand at her waist.

"Just a minute there, darlin'."

Iris shrank away, embarrassed. "I'm sorry."

"There's nothing you need to be sorry for." Those full lips tightened like they had back at the table. "I think that's your husband's job."

She couldn't hold back her snort. "Kirk, apologize? Not in twenty-three years."

His broad hand came up, one finger catching the tear that had escaped without her knowledge. "Maybe if he had learned, it wouldn't have come to this."

She had no response, just shook her head. Looking around, she realized they were in a back hall instead of at the front door as she'd expected. "What—"

"I thought you might prefer some privacy until your ride gets here." He jerked his chin at the door in front of him. "This is my office."

She hesitated, nodded. As she followed him into the room, she noticed the sign on the door. *MANAGER.*

Oh God. She remembered now. The man who'd rescued her was the manager and owner of the Carousel, Jamie

Worthington. She'd seen him at a couple of official functions she and Kirk had attended as members of the Black Wolf's Bluff City Council. And if she kept her seat, she'd likely see him at future events. The man who had overheard the most humiliating moments of her life. The man who had watched and listened as her husband informed her he wanted to cheat on her.

Would this embarrassment follow her for the rest of her life?

"Have a seat." Jamie gestured toward a comfortable looking sofa lining one wall. He took the chair behind the desk, which he swiveled around to the side so nothing obstructed her view of him. "I called Daniel. He should be here in a few."

Daniel ran the only taxi service based in Black Wolf's Bluff. Of course this man would remember her, remember where she came from. She and Kirk were fairly prominent in local politics.

"Thank you." She found herself looking anywhere but at him.

"He's wrong, you know."

She jerked her gaze back to him. Was Jamie flirting with her? Now? But all she read in the man's eyes was sincerity. The hard knot in her gut relaxed the slightest bit. "About what?"

"What he asked you." He leaned back, crossed one ankle over the opposite knee. "Any man you belong to would never need another woman."

The *you belong to* sent a shiver down her spine, though she wasn't certain why. She had no idea how to respond, what to say. They sat in awkward silence for long minutes until Jamie's cell phone chimed. "There is your ride."

She stood and followed him through the halls until they reached the back door. Stepping out, she saw Daniel's blue and white taxi parked by the curb. He flashed his lights in acknowledgment.

She spun quickly and gave Jamie the best smile she could muster, which wasn't saying much. "I appreciate your help, Mr. Worthington."

"Jamie, please." He reached for her hand, held it gently when she accepted his grasp. "You take care, all right?"

Her shaky smile faltered, but she nodded anyway. "Good night."

As she crossed the distance to the cab, she pushed thoughts of Kirk and Jamie and everything else about her night away and walked into her future.

Alone.

Two

"It might be early, but I definitely need a drink."

Scarlett didn't argue, just nodded as they followed Adrian toward a booth at the back of Casa Blanca. At least it was a Saturday. Iris didn't have to go back to work after this; Ashley covered the evening and weekend shifts at the library, and they were closed on Sundays. After what she'd just learned, she definitely wanted a margarita, food, and to go home and bury her head under the covers, in that order.

Kirk was getting remarried. They hadn't even been divorced for three months.

Once they were settled in their seats and Adrian had gone to fill their drink orders, Scarlett reached across the table to take Iris's hand. "I'm sorry to be the bearer of such bad news."

Iris shrugged, the casual move belying the anger churning inside of her. She was grateful for her friend's empathy. "It isn't your fault my ex is an asshole." Or that Scarlett had happened to run into the *lovely couple* in Wildwoods Brew this morning. Kirk had taken the opportunity to make certain Scarlett knew of the impending nuptials, likely because he recognized that the news would travel to Iris forthwith. They'd barely finished sorting and dividing *their entire lives* together—or she had, since Kirk, as usual, had left the emotional baggage for her to carry while he evidently *carried on* with something else—and now he was engaged to a woman twenty years younger than him? Just the thought of dating had nausea tangling her stomach in knots. But then, she imagined Kirk had been dating far longer than she even wanted to think about.

It was that thought that burst the bubble of her anger, sinking her back into the grief and exhaustion that had been her mainstay for the past few months. Unlike him, she hadn't had any forewarning of the divorce, or not any that she truly recognized. She'd had to do all her working through of the emotions in the past six months instead. And God, was she tired of it all.

She sighed, rubbing at her aching eyes. "I just can't believe it."

When she dropped her hands, it was to face Scarlett's stare, heavy with concern. That look made Iris squirm in her seat.

"It's not that I want him back; you know that, right?" Just the thought made her self-conscious. Women shouldn't miss cheaters, though whether Kirk had physically cheated on her or not, she had never been certain. He'd said he wanted an open marriage; he'd never admitted to already seeing someone else, likely so he wouldn't jeopardize the divorce settlement. Not that that had helped him in any significant way. They'd been married over two decades; she'd gotten half of literally everything.

"Of course you don't want that bastard back," Scarlett agreed.

"I do miss…" She focused on the table, her thumb tracing a scar in the worn wood. Admitting she missed anything was hard, even with friends she knew wouldn't judge her. "I miss the man he used to be, the one who was by my side for so many years when the kids were young. This Kirk"—she waved a vague hand—"he's a stranger. I sat across the table from him that night and realized I didn't know him at all."

The separation had been like tearing her flesh apart—how did you divide a lifetime of memories and connections and sheer *stuff*? Selling the house had been one thing, but what was inside... And of course Kirk hadn't made a single damn decision. *She'd* had to present him a list of things she wanted to take with her. *She'd* had to decide how to equitably split things that were too small for the list, like kitchen utensils and pantry items. *She'd* had to divide up the photo albums and Christmas ornaments into hers, his, and their kids'.

The whole thing had been done in the three months it took to finalize the divorce. She'd spent the past three months dealing with the sorrow left behind, setting up her "new life," getting some frigging sleep. But it didn't matter how much she slept; she still felt tired.

"A midlife crisis does many a man in," Scarlett was saying.

Iris snorted. Wasn't that right?

The drinks arrived with perfect timing. Relief fizzled through her. "Thanks, Adrian."

The waiter gave her a wink. "Let me know if you want a top up."

Scarlett giggled as the young man walked away. "Is he a mind-reader?"

"Hopefully. He gets it from his mama." Adrian was the son of Wildwood Brews' owner, Maria.

Iris gripped her glass, raised it to touch Scarlett's, and put on her bravest face. "To Kirk not being my problem anymore." The divorce may have been final three months ago, but having Kirk tied to another woman broke Iris's ties to him in a way a piece of paper couldn't really match. She

11

felt the separation deep inside, a finality nothing else had come close to touching.

Scarlett's grin was sympathetic. "Amen to that. Freedom!"

Iris squared her shoulders and took a drink. *Freedom* was a bittersweet word, but one she was determined to embrace.

Adrian kept her glass refilled—maybe a little too well, Iris realized an hour later when she turned her head to thank him for taking her plate and the room spun. "Wow."

Scarlett giggled. "What?"

"I think Abril is making the drinks stronger than usual for lunchtime."

"Or maybe we've had a few too many." Scarlett shrugged. "That's okay; Gavin will come pick us up. He's hanging with Carter and Thad over at Erin's."

Thad was out of school for the summer; she remembered that now. Had it really already been six months since Scarlett had met Gavin and been whisked off her feet? Sadness washed over Iris at the realization. She missed her best friend when she was away.

"Hey," Scarlett whispered across the table. "No getting maudlin over there."

Iris shook away the depression. "Why would you think I was getting 'maudlin'?" Such a silly word. She was the one who giggled this time.

"Because I know you and that look on your face."

She screwed said face into a funny expression aimed in her friend's direction. "What look?"

"The maudlin look."

That didn't tell her anything. She rolled her eyes. "I—"

The trilling of Scarlett's phone interrupted her. Iris recognized the ringtone that indicated the message was from Gavin. Scarlett glanced at the screen, and her cheeks took on a bright pink tone.

"What?"

Scarlett's brows lifted, a laugh escaping her as she clicked on Gavin's message. The laugh choked off as she read.

"Oh Lord."

"What?" Iris asked again, her voice the slightest bit taunting. As if she didn't know what. Only one thing would have Scarlett's face turning that embarrassing shade of red.

Scarlett screwed her eyes shut for a moment before glancing at Iris. "It's Gavin."

"I know; I recognize the ringtone."

A wry smile twisted Scarlett's lips. "He's feeling…" She seemed to search for just the right word, finally settling on, "Playful."

Iris just bet he was. Melancholy curled through her.

"Hey." Scarlett left her seat to come around to Iris's side of the booth, forcing her to scoot farther in. Her friend placed a warm arm around her, and the relief of having someone comfort her, of not having to be the strong one right now, nearly did her in.

"What's wrong?" Scarlett whispered, keeping their conversation just between the two of them.

"I'm tired, Scarlett. I'm just…" She wiped her hand over her wet eyes and wondered if this was what divorce did to women, made them emotional drunks. "I'm just tired. I feel tired. Hell"—she gestured into the air vaguely—"I even look tired. I look in the mirror and wonder who that woman is staring back at me."

It was as if she'd been unmoored after a quarter of a decade being tied securely in place, and now she didn't know how to get herself back to safety. On the worst days, she didn't feel like she had the strength to try.

Scarlett gave her shoulders a squeeze. Her friend looked at her, really looked, and Iris knew she was being seen. "Do you think this is a reaction to the news?"

"Kirk's news?" When Scarlett nodded, Iris sighed. "I don't think so." She'd been feeling this way for weeks. She thought she'd finally gotten through the grief of having a part of her life cut off, but the aftermath wasn't much better, at least when she allowed herself to acknowledge it. Apparently alcohol broke down all the barriers she'd put up.

Scarlett bumped their shoulders together. "So hanging with me isn't exciting enough to pull you out of the doldrums?"

Iris smiled, trying to hide the return of her sadness, still lingering inside. "'Doldrums'? Do people really say 'doldrums'?"

Scarlett shrugged. "Hey, words are my thing."

They certainly were; Scarlett was a great writer. But getting back to Scarlett's question… "When you're here," she admitted, hoping her lack of spite came through. The situation was what it was. "You spend as much time in Scotland as you do in Tennessee now."

Scarlett sighed. "I know. I'm sorry."

"Why?"

"Because all of this hit at the same time."

"That wasn't your fault." Just because Kirk had chosen to blow things up right before Christmas didn't mean Scarlett should regret meeting Gavin. The Scotsman made her friend ecstatically happy. "The two of you are perfect together. That's something to celebrate."

"Oh, I do." Scarlett grinned. "Gavin makes sure of it every time he gets me in bed."

Iris barely refrained from wincing. Of all the things she missed about marriage, sex and the intimacy it provided were at the top of the list.

Scarlett gave her another hug, her mood turning serious once more. "I do wish I could be here for you more."

"I miss you when you're gone"—Iris squared her shoulders—"but I'm a big girl."

Scarlett returned to her seat, and they ordered sopapillas to share. They were halfway through dessert when Scarlett narrowed her eyes on Iris in a way that had her once more squirming in her seat. "You know…"

Her friend's tone had alarms going off in Iris's brain. "Know what?"

"I've been thinking—"

"Dangerous," Iris said into her margarita glass.

"Would you stop interrupting me?"

Iris giggled. Uh-oh. Maybe dessert hadn't soaked up as much of the alcohol as she'd thought. Gavin was definitely going to need to pick them up.

"I was wondering," Scarlett said, "how about a date? Maybe you need to get out more."

Her knee-jerk reaction—aside from wanting to throw up—was, "Absolutely not. I have no desire to start dating for a long, long time." Unlike Kirk. "If ever," she added. She still stumbled when she called him her ex. Just because he was planning to jump from their marriage into another within six months didn't mean she wanted to.

Sure, her life got lonely. She went from work at the library to her tiny apartment and back to work, with a stop at the store or a night out with the girls or lunch with her daughter as a rare schedule interrupter. Routine had helped her adapt at first, but the monotony was starting to get to her. That didn't mean she wanted to add someone else to her mess.

"Why not?" Scarlett frowned. "It doesn't have to be anything serious."

"No." She shuddered. "I haven't dated in, what, twenty-three years?" Dates with Kirk didn't count; she'd stopped her futile attempts to impress him years ago. Maybe if she hadn't…

She slammed that thought down. What had happened had not been about her.

Scarlett was still frowning, but Iris was adamant on this point. No dating.

But when her friend opened her mouth, what came out was, "How about a makeover?"

"A makeover?"

"Yes!" Scarlett bounced in her seat as excitement fizzed up inside her, as visible as bubbles in a champagne glass. "How you're feeling goes deeper than something a new dress or a new pair of shoes could fix. What you need is a new outlook. A new *look*." She raised her brow suggestively. "That's exactly what you need. A facial, a new brand of makeup, maybe some clothes, a haircut."

"My hair?" She fingered the ends of her below-shoulder-length, thick mane. Though it was gray, she was lucky it hadn't faded into that brassy tone some older women got. Veins of pure white and a deep slate enriched the color, making her hair one of the few things she loved about herself at this stage of her life. "What about my hair?"

Scarlett's excitement wasn't waning, but her attention was. She waved off Iris's concerns as she picked up her phone again and tapped to wake up the screen. "Don't worry, Iris; we won't ruin your hair."

She hoped to God not. "So what *are* we going to do? And what do you mean, 'we'?"

Scarlett paused in her typing. "That depends. Is that a yes?"

"Um…" Was it?

She paused, taking a deep look inside at how she'd felt the past few weeks.

Why not? What did she have to lose besides a day of pampering? She didn't have to let them cut her hair if she decided not to. "Okay, yes."

Scarlett let out a whoop, making Iris jump. "I've got just the thing." She returned to texting.

By the time Scarlett set her phone back down, doubts were settling in. "Scarlett, I don't know—"

The phone rang, cutting her off. Scarlett answered. "Lily?

Yeah. Come over to Casa Blanca. Yeah, bring her." She hung up. "Lily and Erin are on their way."

Nerves fluttered in Iris's throat. "To do what?"

"We've got plans to make." Scarlett's grin was downright giddy. "Are you ready?"

"God, no." She smiled wryly. But she did want a change, didn't she? Scarlett was right: she needed a new outlook to go with her new life. Maybe then she could grow her way out of this morass of grief. If Scarlett and the others wanted to help, now was the time to go after it. Time to put her big-girl panties on, so to speak. "I will be ready, though. Let's do this."

Three

She was still the prettiest thing he'd ever laid eyes on, despite the fact that he'd first seen her a decade ago. Jamie knew his smile was strained with worry, but it was genuine—as he watched the pure black mare circle her stall, his heart felt tight in his chest. She'd stolen it the moment she was foaled ten years ago, and he figured she'd own it till the day they reluctantly parted. Though the filly she would give birth to any day now—her first, as her two previous breedings had produced colts—might just take a piece of it as well.

The walkie-talkie attached to his belt crackled. "Sir?"

His mouth quirked, a chuckle escaping. If foaling was unpredictable, Marilyn was the exact opposite. He'd told her from her first day working for him to call him Jamie, but his housekeeper had her own ideas about what was proper. He unclipped the walkie and pressed the button. "Here, Marilyn."

Baby meandered toward the door to her stall at the sound of his voice. He cupped her muzzle, enjoying the softness of her sable coat as he waited for a response. Not that he needed to—he knew what Marilyn was going to say, just as she knew what his reply would be.

"Ms. Deveraux has arrived."

"Perfect." He ran his thumb firmly back and forth along Baby's cheek, just as she liked. "Have Harris bring her down to the barn, please."

"Of course, sir."

Shaking his head at the woman's stubbornness, he replaced the walkie in its holster and continued to give Baby the comfort she sought. The mare was uncomfortable; he could see it in her eyes, in the way she lifted her head over the gate and rested her forehead against his chest, her breath blowing gently against his stomach.

"Just a few more days, darlin'. It won't be long and the little one will be here."

As if she knew exactly what he was saying, the horse gave a huge sigh. He switched to rubbing her ears. They stayed that way for long minutes until the sound of an ATV crunching through the gravel drew near.

With what he swore was a long-suffering *harumph*, Baby backed into her stall. Eyeing her hay, he gauged how much she had left before turning toward his morning visitor. "Erin, welcome to the farm! I'm sorry you had to come all this way."

His general contractor slid from the back of the vehicle. Walking through the wide doorway to the barn, she rubbed her rounded belly. Her face was lit with that glow only pregnancy gave a woman. "Nonsense. I'm on my feet all day, and when I'm up at Black Wolf's Bluff, it's all uphill. A ride down to your place is a welcome change."

Jamie gave Harris, one of the longtime hands that helped run the ranch, a nod of thanks before reaching for Erin. A quick kiss to her cheek had become his signature greeting despite their business relationship. He'd grown to genuinely like and care for the woman, her husband, Carter, and their son, Thad, over the past year. Erin was not only the best contractor around in his opinion, but the best kind of human being, and he was proud to call her a friend.

"You, my dear, are absolutely radiant."

"Am I? I feel a little bit like I swallowed a beach ball and waddle better than most penguins."

He laughed. "Nonsense. There's nothing more beautiful than a pregnant woman." He led her inside out of the sun. "The vet is due this morning, and I didn't want to miss her," he explained, though he'd already told Erin the same thing on the phone. "I appreciate you coming."

Erin waved away the words and wandered over to the gate to Baby's pen. "Is this the troublemaker?"

He chuckled. "Erin, meet Daddy's Girl, or as I affectionately call her, Baby."

Erin wiggled her brows, her focus on the sleek black mare with the bulging belly moving curiously toward her across the stall. "Daddy's Girl, huh?"

"The minute I saw her wobbling around on shaky legs, fresh from her mother's womb, I couldn't call her anything else," he admitted.

Erin grinned. "Some lucky woman would swoon if you called her that, you know."

He swore a blush heated his cheeks; damn his Irish ancestors for passing down their redheaded complexion. Luckily Erin was focused on offering Baby her fingers for a sniff. "I would be the lucky one."

Erin threw him a warm look over her shoulder. "And that right there is what makes you the most eligible bachelor in Gatlinburg."

"Don't remind me," he groaned. Last year the city council held an auction for charity and solicited Jamie for a donation. At the suggestion of some of his (mostly female) staff at the Carousel, he'd offered a date night out on the town, purely platonic. Needless to say, he'd been dubbed "Gatlinburg's Most Eligible Bachelor" ever since.

Erin never missed an opportunity to tease him about that.

"I'm too old to be the most eligible bachelor around," he groused good-naturedly. He'd hit fifty-eight on his last birthday. Far too close to sixty for his liking.

"Hey." Erin gave him a mock frown. "I'm proof age has nothing to do with anything when it comes to love."

He'd guess she was somewhere in her midforties and having her first child. He didn't know her full history, although he did know she'd been a widow for years before meeting Carter and marrying earlier this year. He guessed if she could have a baby, he shouldn't give up on matters of the heart.

The image of a certain lovely woman walking away from him across the Carousel's back parking lot flashed into his mind.

Don't think about it, Worthington. It's way too soon.

The one woman to interest him in forever, and she'd been married—emphasis on the past tense, thank God. Even so, a handful of months wasn't near long enough for Iris Daniels to recover from the blow her husband had dealt her that night, the bastard. Jamie's only consolation was that Kirk Daniels had left Black Wolf's Bluff's sexy-as-hell librarian open to the playing field, so to speak. Eventually, anyway. Jamie felt like he was chomping at the bit, but he'd sworn to give her time to heal before seeking her out. He of all people understood the importance of healing.

He cleared his throat. "You had some supplier issues you wanted to discuss?"

Erin took the hint and got down to business, intermingled with crooning and caresses for Baby. The mare ate up the attention until more crunching gravel outside signaled the arrival of the veterinarian.

As Baby pulled her head back into the stall and moved away, Erin threw a glance over Jamie's shoulder. "I can go and leave y'all to it."

He closed his phone on his notes, shaking his head. "We've still got to go over that change in the architect's plan for the upstairs restrooms." A jerk of his head indicated a bench nearby. "Why don't you take a load off while I talk with the doc?"

"Don't you mean harass the doc for answers she can't possibly give you?" Dr. Everest asked, stepping into the dim light of the barn.

Jamie scoffed. "I haven't been that bad."

Laura Everest eyed him like he'd been replaced with an alien. "You haven't?"

Behind her, Harris chuckled, quickly muffling the sound with his hand. Jamie did his best to look offended without laughing. Laura loved giving him a hard time. "I'm just worried."

Shaking her head, the vet shot him an incredulous look as she arrived at Baby's stall. "Right. Why aren't you this worried when I come out to treat any other horse?"

Because Baby is special. "I worry," he said again, voice gruff.

"About that one especially," Harris said with a jerk of his head toward the favored one, who nickered as if she knew exactly whom they were all discussing.

"Don't you have something you could be doing?" Jamie asked his ranch hand.

Laura laughed. Behind Jamie, Erin joined in. Harris backed out of the barn, shaking his head good-naturedly. Jamie gave them all his best scowl.

"Everyone knows you're a pushover for this mare, Worthington," the vet said, grinning. "But that's okay; I like you all the better for it."

Refraining from an answer, he unhooked the door to Baby's stall and waved Laura inside. Baby's snort of displeasure told him she knew exactly why the doc was here, but she stood quietly as Laura examined her. Finally, anxious minutes later, Laura gave the mare a soft pat on the belly and declared, "Everything's looking good."

Jamie breathed a sigh of relief.

Laura gathered up her equipment. "I'm thinking she has a week at least, maybe ten days. Mama and baby are both doing well."

"You're sure about the time frame? I've got to be in Nashville tomorrow, and I hate being that far away when she could go at any time."

The vet shook her head. "You know as well as I do that these things are unpredictable, but I'm giving you my best guess. You're safe, don't worry." Laura slapped him on the back on her way past. "She'll be fine, Daddy."

Erin raised an amused eyebrow behind the vet's back but refrained from comment. Jamie silently gave thanks.

He walked Laura out to the path leading back to the house, thanking her for coming. When he re-entered the barn, Erin had her shoulder propped against the door to Baby's stall, the black horse nuzzling the long brown braid that hung over Erin's shoulder. Jamie pulled his phone back out to retrieve his notes.

After a thorough discussion of the architect's recommendations, Jamie put his phone away again. "You know," Erin said, her tone casual, "if you're going to be in Nashville tomorrow, you should stick around and meet Carter and me at Bourbon & Bone for dinner. We could check out the competition."

His smirk matched hers. "You know as well as I do that there's no competition for the Carousel." He'd built the best restaurant possible from a foundation of nothing, and the success they'd enjoyed through the years proved it. The Carousel was *the* go-to location for hours around. "Besides, I don't want to be the third wheel for your date night."

Erin waved away his words. "Don't worry about that. Several of us are going. The girls and I are having a spa day in

Nashville, and Carter and JD are meeting us tomorrow night. Linc is out of town filming, and Gavin had to make a quick run to New York for business, so they can't join us. But we figured if we're going all that way, might as well enjoy ourselves." She chuckled as Baby lipped curiously at her hair. "You should come."

By this time Jamie was familiar with Erin's circle of friends, which included some of the most prominent people in Black Wolf's Bluff—and one in particular that he'd had his eye on. Feeling like he was back in high school, nosing around his friends for a particular girl's whereabouts, he asked, "Iris wouldn't happen to be joining you, would she?"

At Erin's knowing look, Jamie silently cursed. "She would." A sly grin appeared. He barely held back a groan. "Iris is definitely joining us."

"Erin…"

She shook her head at his warning tone, actually giggling like a schoolgirl. "Nope, there's no backing out now. You just let me in on a little secret, and you get to reap the consequences."

She was practically rubbing her hands together with glee. He dragged a rough palm down his face. "Lord."

"Yep," she quipped. "Be prepared."

Did she have to sound so happy about it? He looked down at his friend, amused, but then his mood shifted toward the serious. In for a penny, right? "I don't care what you say about me, but I don't want Iris to be uncomfortable. She's been through enough already." He didn't know what all Iris had told her friends about the reason for her divorce and he'd never tell tales about what he'd witnessed, but word around town was that the divorce had been a messy affair. Not because of Iris, but because of her lousy husband.

Erin's gaze softened, and she squeezed his biceps. "You're a good man, Jamie."

The words tightened his chest. He shook his head. "She's a

good woman. She deserves the time out without me being foisted on her." Still, a desire to throw caution to the wind and jump on this chance was rearing its ugly head inside him.

Erin turned toward the opening of the barn, throwing a wink over her shoulder. "Trust me. You I'd make uncomfortable all day long"—she laughed—"but not Iris. Just come. You won't regret it."

He hoped not, because damn his hide, but he couldn't pass up the opportunity to bring himself to Iris's attention once again. He only prayed she could forgive him for being present tomorrow night, a reminder of things she'd probably rather forget. If she gave him the chance, he'd replace that unhappy memory with ones he hoped she'd never want to erase.

Four

A week after her lunch with Scarlett, Iris walked into an upscale salon in Nashville with a small posse of women at her side. Somehow having Erin, Lily, and Claire along with Scarlett made Iris feel more like she had an audience than a support group, which was silly because every woman with her was a hundred percent committed to providing encouragement along her journey toward her "new outlook." Still, butterflies felt like they were swarming in her throat as well as her stomach.

She pulled Scarlett to one side in the lobby. "I know I said I was ready for this, but…" Her voice petered out.

The look she gave her friend must've been desperate, because Scarlett wrapped an arm around her and pulled her into a hug scented with her favorite coconut body spray. "It's gonna be fine. Trust me, Iris. Lily said this place is the absolute best."

Iris's stomach cramped. "Best for whom?" she asked under her breath.

Lily must've heard her, because the woman's musical laughter surrounded them. "For you, of course," she said, squeezing Iris's shoulder reassuringly as Scarlett released her.

"Just remember, this is a day to pamper yourself. You don't have to let Jose do anything you aren't comfortable with." Lily leaned in a bit closer as they restarted their journey toward the front desk. "But I will tell you, he has great instincts."

Great instincts. That would be helpful, since all her instincts were screaming in fear. She'd had the same "look" for a couple of decades, and that look had served her fine. Stepping into the unknown...

"Ms. Daniels?"

She jerked to a stop in front of the glossy gold reception desk. *Stop being a ninny!* Iris squared her shoulders and mustered her warmest smile for the woman behind the desk. "Yes. Iris Daniels."

"Lovely! I'm Emme"—she pointed to the name tag pinned to the deep green, silky shirt that matched the silk-covered wall behind her—"and I'll be getting you started this morning." Rounding the desk, she offered each of them an eager smile. "We're having a girls' day? You ladies will be walking out of here happy, relaxed, and lovely this afternoon."

Iris definitely hoped so.

"Let's begin with a drink, shall we?"

Relief had Iris's shoulders dropping from around her ears. "Yes, please." A chorus of agreements came from the rest of their group, all except Erin, who added, "And a lemon water, please. My ankles are doing their best impression of an elephant's this morning."

Emme chuckled—discreetly, of course—as she led them across the lobby. The room she escorted them into had soft cream walls uplit with warm light that highlighted the multitude of lush plants dotting the area. Low music enhanced the relaxed ambience, as did the pretty peach blush of the mimosas Emme handed out. Each woman was given a locker and a luxurious robe and a few minutes to change. By the time Iris rejoined the group, everyone but Erin was chilling in the plush loungers scattered about, fluffy robes and socks wrapping them in warmth, half-empty drinks in hand.

Iris set her mimosa on the small table next to an empty seat. As she settled into the lounger, the door to the locker room opened and Erin walked in, tugging her robe tightly over her rounded belly. "This kid is becoming a problem," she groused, her half-smile telling them all she wasn't as upset with her figure as she might sound.

Iris gave her a conciliatory look, remembering the uncomfortable days of her own two pregnancies like they were yesterday. "So much emphasis is placed on both staying skinny *and* having kids. Kind of contradictory, isn't it?"

Erin retrieved her sparkling water from the nearby cart, rubbing her opposite hand over her baby mound. "Definitely." She glanced down, her smile indulgent. "She's totally worth every second that my clothes don't want to fit, though." As she sat, she tugged at her robe once more, hiding the peek of skin that was revealed as the fabric crept open. "It just hits me at the weirdest times."

"How many children do you have, Iris?" Lily asked. "I know you have a daughter."

"Yes. Krista." Iris's smile was indulgent this time. "She works in the Sevier County archives office." She stopped for a drink. "My son is a judicial clerk in Seattle. He fell in love with the Pacific Northwest on a trip in college and was determined to move there as soon as he finished law school." Both her children were doing something they loved, and she couldn't be more proud.

They chatted about family a bit, Iris enjoying the time getting to know Lily, Erin, and Claire a bit more personally than she had been able to during noisy evenings at the Drunken Otter or short lunches on a weekday. One by one each of her friends was collected by an attendant until Iris was the last one waiting. Just as she finished her second mimosa, the door to the back of the salon opened and a slim man walked inside, followed by a small team of assistants. Iris's eyes went wide.

"Ms. Daniels? I'm Jose." He flashed her a warm smile that lit up his handsome face. "May I call you Iris? We'll be spending a lot of time together today."

She'd known she was assigned to Jose; she hadn't realized he would come with an entourage. Her nerves began a second, thankfully milder tap dance in her belly. "Of course." She moved to stand, but the stylist waved her back into her seat, perching instead on the end of the lounger next to her.

"So I hear you are interested in a new look."

Her fingers found their way to the ends of her hair without conscious thought. "I don't know about a *new* look," she admitted, feeling more than a little uncertain now that the time was here. "I was hoping to, you know, freshen *my* look up a bit."

The way Jose was eyeing her hair could only be called greedy. "I would love to help you with that. Here's what I'm thinking."

By the time he'd outlined his plan, excitement and terror were warring for supremacy in her stomach. Yes, she'd wanted something different, a fresh start, so to speak, but what Jose was proposing…

As if he recognized the fear in her eyes, he patted her hand where it lay on the arm of the lounger, giving her a friendly squeeze. "Trust me. I promise, you're going to love looking in the mirror every day when I'm done with you."

Had she ever loved looking in the mirror every day? For special occasions, maybe, but otherwise she was just Iris and had been for forever. Frankly, wearing a sexy Halloween costume was the closest she'd gotten to true enjoyment in her looks in years. And suddenly, fiercely she wanted to experience that all over again.

Bracing her shoulders against her nerves, she gave Jose a nod. "Okay, let's do it."

"Great." He rubbed his hands together, his anticipation stoking Iris's enthusiasm even more. "Let's get going, people."

While his team laid the groundwork for Iris's "transformation," Jose sent her off with a masseuse whose hands were pure magic. If Iris had been nervous before the massage, after it, she was literally putty in Jose's hands. A deep conditioner was applied to her hair—no artificial color, Jose said, could ever compare to the natural glorious shades that made up her hair color, a statement that made Iris preen a bit—and while it did its work, Jose's team did theirs, tackling a pedicure, manicure, and facial all at once. Lunch came after, which she spent giggling through finger foods with her friends, before a wardrobe selection was presented for her to try. And try she did, with Lily, Erin, Scarlett, and Claire chiming in until they settled on a slim black dress that played up Iris's ivory locks and showed off slender, muscled legs she'd always been proud of. Already she felt ten years younger, but now came the hard part.

Her hair.

Not that Jose's ideas didn't sound fabulous, but her hair… How could she describe her feelings about it? So many women her age cut their hair into classic—boring!—bobs or shoulder-length, shapeless masses. She'd always felt rather smug about her long, thick hair. But at the end of the day, after Jose had snipped and shaped, his assistant had artfully applied sexy makeup, and the subtly sensual black dress was on her body, one look in the mirror told her Jose had been correct—the new cut made her love looking in the mirror. She adored it!

"Wow!" A wolf whistle sounded behind her. She turned to see Erin grinning at Iris's reflection in the mirror.

"Holy shit, Iris," Scarlett exclaimed, coming to her side. The quartet of ladies surrounded her, all staring as raptly into the mirror as she had been. Scarlett reached up to finger Iris's short hair. "That's the sexiest haircut I've ever seen—and I never even considered haircuts sexy on a woman."

Snickers escaped each of them, and Scarlett stuck her tongue out at them all. Iris turned her attention back to the mirror. Funny or not, Scarlett wasn't wrong. Her thick hair was cropped close to her head in a shaggy style that gave her a modern edge. The top and front were longer, showcasing the depth of the layers, and a long length of curls fell over one eye, adding mystery and, dare she say it, a touch of whimsy she absolutely loved. Her dark brows winged over her gray eyes, a sharp contrast to the pale tones in her hair. Black cat's-eye glasses framed her eyes, giving her a sensual look she'd never thought she'd attribute to her quiet self.

"Gives a whole new meaning to the term 'sexy librarian,' doesn't it?" Lily observed. Her wink at Iris's reflection made Iris's cheeks go pink.

"Right?" Scarlett agreed.

"You were attractive before," Claire said, her dark eyes twinkling, "but damn, Iris!"

"Tell me how you really feel," Iris teased the younger woman.

Everyone laughed. Her friends exclaimed over her makeup, her dress, the glittery gold heels on her feet, every last detail of her "transformation" until Emme came in to announce that a car had arrived to pick them up. Iris lingered at the mirror a moment longer, reveling in the delight that filled her at the woman staring back at her, the exciting realization that the woman was *her*, before rushing to gather her things.

Dinner was waiting, and suddenly she was starving.

Five

Jamie reached to grasp JD's hand for a firm shake as the two men met on the threshold of Bourbon & Bone. Lily Easton Lane's husband had caused quite the uproar when he arrived in Black Wolf's Bluff last year, planning to develop his family property. So much uproar they'd even heard about it in Gatlinburg. Jamie had met the man more than once at local civic events, not to mention hosting the rehearsal dinner for the couple's Christmas wedding a few months ago.

"Glad you could join us," JD said. "It's nice to have a bit more testosterone at the table."

Jamie grinned. "Hey, I'm just here to bask in the estrogen."

Carter, Erin's husband, also shook his hand. "Aren't we all?"

The three men were escorted to a primo table near the back, a round booth perfect for large groups. Jamie listened with half an ear to Carter's enthusiasm over Erin's plans for their new house in New York, one eye on the door, waiting for Iris's appearance. His chest ached like he was holding his breath, and butterflies were lighting up his stomach. As uncomfortable as the sensations were, he also relished them—

he hadn't felt this invested in a woman in a long while. A very long while. Of course, Iris may not have given him a second thought once she stepped into the cab behind the Carousel that night, but if she hadn't, he was damn well determined to bring himself to her attention now.

And then she walked through the door.

Jamie's breath stopped. It was the Iris he'd expected, except so much more. Her long hair had been cut short, and new glasses framed her eyes with a sexy uptilt. And that dress... He'd known she had a great figure, tall and curvy, but the black dress she wore showcased that fact, leaving him in zero doubt as to whether or not she was perfect for him—absolutely perfect.

"There they are."

Carter's voice broke the spell that had Jamie in its hold. Hastily he stood, feeling a helluva lot younger and unsure of himself in the face of this woman he wanted so much. He didn't like the feeling—he wasn't the kind of man who doubted himself. With Iris, well, there was so much at risk. So much he wanted.

But was she ready?

"Ladies!" JD moved straight to Lily, taking his wife in his arms for a kiss. Carter greeted his wife similarly, leaving Jamie facing Iris and Scarlett unimpeded.

"Ladies." Jamie repeated JD's greeting, but his voice was rough, husky. Iris hesitated at the edge of the space around the booth, her friend Scarlett at her side. The grin Scarlett was giving him said she'd been let in on Erin's little invitation and the reason for it.

"Hello." It was Scarlett who replied. Iris remained silent, feeling awkward if her expression was anything to go by. He hoped his smile would help put her at ease, although he feared the heat he felt as he focused on her could not be hidden.

Erin pulled back from Carter and turned to them. "Iris,

Scarlett, do you know Jamie Worthington? We're working together on the building of his new restaurant."

"We've met." Scarlett extended her hand. "At the rehearsal dinner for JD and Lily, I believe."

He shook hands with her, searching his memory until it landed on the fact that she was a writer. "You're the local author."

"I am." Her smile lit up her eyes, telling him how much she loved her work.

A hint of mischief appeared too, and he saw Scarlett nudge her shoulder against Iris's back. Jamie centered his focus on the woman he'd come to see. "Iris, I believe?" As if he didn't know her name as well as his own. "Call me Jamie."

"Hello again, Jamie." Iris's voice was as hesitant as her body, but her words, his name on her lips, told him all he needed to know. She'd thought about him, all right. She remembered, and the tone of her voice, however tentative, wasn't unfriendly.

Determination filled him alongside the knowledge. He moved to meet her, take her hands in his. She gasped at his touch as if surprised—or maybe she felt the same zing of pleasure as he did. He held her gaze as long as he could, bending forward to brush a kiss along her cheek. "It's a pleasure to see you again."

Her fingers tightened on his at the touch of his lips. When he pulled back, a flustered look greeted him. Wanting to give her time to settle—and wanting to continue touching her—he turned toward the booth and slid his hand around to rest at the small of her back. "Have a seat."

It took a few moments to gather everyone into their places, but when all was settled, he was exactly where he wanted to be: right next to Iris, his arm brushing hers, his knee skimming her thigh as he turned in her direction. The scent of citrus and warm woman filled his nose, and he breathed deep, committing Iris's essence to memory.

"I can't wait to try the food here," Claire was saying. "Lincoln has talked about this place several times, but we haven't managed to squeeze in the stop."

Her...fiancé, maybe? This group's relationship statuses were difficult to keep track of, but he thought that was right. Lincoln Young was a well-known chef who knew his food. Jamie agreed—he'd eaten here several times, and it never ceased to make his mouth water with anticipation. "I highly recommend the rib eye. Perfectly aged, everything a steak should be."

Iris looked to him. "You've been here before."

He shrugged. "Investors expect the best." He dared a wink. "And I love good food."

He swore a blush darkened her cheeks, though the dim lighting of the restaurant made it difficult to tell for certain. She turned her attention back to her menu, and he made a discreet adjustment below the rim of the table, hoping for a bit more breathing room in his slacks.

Once they had placed their orders—Iris ordered the filet mignon, which he'd also recommended as excellent—conversation around the table turned toward the afternoon of pampering, Carter and JD's drive over, the latest updates to Claire's new bakery, the one taking shape brick by brick inside JD's soon-to-be-opened resort. Jamie could feel the tension slowly draining from Iris's body as she relaxed, joined in, and hopefully became used to his body in close proximity to hers.

"Jamie"—Erin's grin had an impish tilt to it—"how was Baby doing this morning?"

Iris froze next to him. Jamie barely resisted the urge to place his hand on her neck, let his touch warm her, reassure her.

"She's hanging in there," he told Erin. "Still looking to foal in the next week."

Iris blew out a breath. The act was subtle; he doubted

anyone else was aware of her reactions, but he was so fine-tuned to her every movement that he couldn't miss them if he'd tried.

"A horse?" she asked. "You have a horse named Baby?"

"I do." He grinned. "Want me to whip out the photos on my phone?"

She laughed. "Tell me about her. She's having a baby? Is she your only horse?"

Erin jumped in. "Jamie owns a farm between Gatlinburg and Black Wolf's Bluff. Flying Horse Ranch? How many horses do you have now?"

He shrugged. "A couple dozen. The number fluctuates between births and the sales we make." He added, for Iris's benefit, "I breed American Quarter Horses."

Something seemed to click into place for her. "And you own the Carousel, right?"

His mouth quirked in a grin. "Right."

Her laugh did strange things to his heart. "'Flying Horse Ranch.' That makes so much sense." She paused as their server arrived with everyone's drinks. "So, how did you get into horse breeding?"

"I moved to the area a good thirty years ago now." Had it really been so long? Time flew when you were getting old, he guessed. "I bought the land because I like my space, and because I wanted horses for pleasure. I never expected to breed them, but I caught the bug with my very first quarter horse and"—he shrugged, a tingle shooting through him as his shoulder contacted Iris's—"the rest is history."

"Was Baby your first?" Iris asked.

He chuckled. "No, that was a bay named Cerberus. Ironic since he was the gentlest gelding I've ever owned. I fell in love with the breed then, slowly built my herd, expanded the farm..." He glanced around, realizing he might be monopolizing the conversation, but the others talked around them, leaving him and Iris in their own little world.

What had he been saying? Oh.

"Baby's official name is Daddy's Girl." He grinned. "She was born ten years ago on the farm, and the minute I laid eyes on her"—his gaze met Iris's, and a sense of déjà vu came over him—"I fell in love."

His voice had gone husky; he couldn't help it. The words hung in the air between them, full of suggestion, until the arrival of the server with their food interrupted them.

The conversation flowed around the table as the group ate, and Jamie took a back seat, wanting to learn more about Iris now that he finally had the chance. He'd caught glimpses at a couple of social functions, civic events where the city council of Black Wolf's Bluff were present, and through the conversations with Erin about her friends, but it wasn't the same as watching Iris actually interact with others, getting to interact with him herself. Those few moments last December had sparked his interest, but tonight opened up a whole different view of the woman beside him, one he both admired and wanted even more than he had before.

Good food and good company had the evening passing far sooner than he wanted it to. As the checks were collected, talk turned to where each couple was headed for the night. JD and Lily needed to drive back to Black Wolf's Bluff in preparation for an early morning meeting Lily couldn't miss. Carter and Erin had a sitter for Thad, and had rented a suite to enjoy some time on their own. Claire, Scarlett, and Iris were all staying in town, at a hotel just down the street, which was also where Jamie had reserved a room. He no longer enjoyed traveling through the night if he didn't have to; better to rest in a nice warm bed and travel the next day, in his opinion. Tonight that decision was a good one for a whole other reason.

"Let me escort you ladies to the hotel."

Erin's wink was discreetly hidden from her friends, and he silently thanked her for suggesting the location for his overnight stay. Hugs were shared all around, and then he found himself walking up the sidewalk with Iris at his side, Scarlett and Claire slightly ahead of them in what he was fairly certain was a strategic plan to give him some alone time with their friend.

Iris shivered at his side. "Cold?" The evening had cooled off significantly after the day's summer heat.

She shot him a wry smile. "Tonight is cooler than I expected."

Without comment he slid his blazer from his shoulders and wrapped it casually around hers. Iris protested even as she snuggled into the collar's warmth.

"No worries," he assured her. "I'm sure if I get too chilly, you'll keep me warm."

He loved the fact that he could provoke that pretty pink color in her cheeks with just the right words.

Iris walked on in silence for a moment, then surprised him by stopping on the sidewalk and turning to face him. "Thank you."

"I told you, I'm fine in the cold."

"Not for that," she said. "For…" She glanced at her friends up ahead, then back at him. "I never got a chance to thank you for that night."

Ah. "You don't have to thank me for that, Iris."

She glanced down at her hands, clutched around her purse. "I do. I—" She seemed to struggle to form the words she wanted, but Jamie waited patiently, wanting to hear them, wanting to know her every thought. "I've never told anyone exactly what Kirk said to me that night. I never wanted anyone to know." She met his eyes, uncertainty in hers. "I hated for a long time that you'd heard them. Hated that anyone knew what he wanted of me."

He stepped close, his hand rising without thought to cup her cheek. "What he wanted is on him, Iris, not you. It's a reflection of his own internal lack." He rubbed his thumb up

38

and down her soft skin. "You are everything you need to be, just as you are."

Her eyes closed, and she leaned into his touch. After a moment her spine stiffened and she opened her eyes. Determination filled them.

"Jamie?"

"Hmm?" Those pretty gray eyes drew him in, stealing his words.

And then she spoke again, and his voice deserted him completely.

"Would you kiss me?"

Six

S he knew she should resist. She'd known from the moment she walked into the restaurant and saw him standing there next to their booth. She'd had too many thoughts about Jamie Worthington since the night she'd left Kirk, and more than one fantasy. His presence endangered the sanity she'd barely managed to stabilize since the divorce.

And still, despite the way her heart stuck in her throat, threatening to strangle the words she wanted to say, she whispered, "Would you kiss me?"

Jamie's eyes went wide, and he hesitated. Embarrassment flooded her. *See? You're not made for dating. Talk about out of practice—you've never been* in practice *at propositioning a man.*

He doesn't want to kiss you.

That's what you get for being so forward.

"I'm sor—"

Before she could finish her apology, he swooped down and his lips met hers.

Iris's breath stopped.

His lips felt unfamiliar. She was so used to... No, she

didn't want to think about him right now. She had asked for this, and she wanted to savor it.

Savor? With sudden alarm she realized she was just standing there as if frozen, unmoving, stiff. What must Jamie think?

You're a ninny. Stop being a ninny. Take the chance while you have it.

She relaxed against him. Without thought her lips parted, just the slightest bit. An invitation. *Come in. Let me taste you.*

Taste me.

Jamie's scent filled her senses—something spicy that she couldn't put a name to but adored nonetheless.

How long had it been since she'd reveled in the scent of a man, in the feel of his body against hers? Too long. Jamie's chest was wide, his body heavyset but not fat. He felt hard, tough, like he could protect her from anything that came their way. She slid her hands against his sides, leaning in until her breasts flattened against his ribs.

And then his tongue breeched her lips.

Sensation zinged from her mouth to her breasts to her core, at once powerful and oh so startling. He tasted of the wine he'd had with dinner, and she opened wider, letting him in, encouraging him to explore. Her tongue tangled with his. Her nipples tightened, and she couldn't suppress the urge to squeeze her legs together, adding pressure where it felt the best.

It had been so long.

Jamie drew back, dived in for another kiss, then drew back again. His breath was heavy as he leaned his forehead against hers. Only then did she realize his hands were gripping her hips much like hers were grasping him, and she basked in his sure hold.

"Jamie." Was that really her voice, all breathless and husky?

"Iris." Jamie's voice was guttural. He tipped his head up,

his lips settling against her forehead. "I've been thinking about that for a long time."

Alarm zinged through her. "You have?"

He chuckled, the sound rumbling through his chest and into her. "Damn right I have."

She leaned back, daring to look him in the eyes, to stroke her palms over his ribs and up his muscular chest. She shouldn't admit what she was thinking, shouldn't give him any more ammunition to use against her, and still the words, "I've thought about it too," slipped out. She had, mostly in moments that caught her unaware. Her dreams especially. Jamie had featured in more than one dream that had left her feeling uncertain and achy. Though she had seen him before then, he had been intrinsically linked to the end of her marriage by his presence at their anniversary dinner. It had somehow seemed wrong to also want him sexually, but she did want him.

That sense of vulnerability surged again. Touching him, wanting him bared her in a way she didn't like. The feeling that she was teetering on the edge of a cliff, about to fall, about to expose herself to the pain that could come with emotion, with opening herself up to another human being, had her drawing back.

She wasn't ready. She didn't think she'd ever be ready.

Pulling her arms away seemed to take tremendous effort —her hands wanted to keep hold of the stability and warmth they'd found in Jamie's body, but for her sanity, she had to deny them. She had to deny him.

"Iris?"

She clutched her arms around herself instead and looked up at this handsome man who made her feel things she no longer felt safe feeling. "Hmm?"

He reached for her, and she flinched. She couldn't help it.

He dropped his hand quickly. "Are you all right?"

"O-of course." She glanced up the street, grateful to see

Scarlett and Claire were not too far ahead. "We'd better catch up."

Jamie overtook her quickly. "What's going through that lovely head of yours?"

His voice sounded concerned. Jamie was an intelligent man, that much she knew. And he seemed to know his way around a woman's brain; he could probably read all the sudden doubts and worries, conjectures and condemnations flooding her mind.

"Everything." An uncomfortable laugh escaped. "Always. I'm a chronic overthinker."

"That fits."

She skidded to a stop. "How does that fit?" As if she didn't know.

Jamie reached for her again, only this time she was too intent on his words. He pulled her back against him. "Most intelligent women are overthinkers. Comes with the territory. Taking everything on yourself. Carrying all the baggage; shouldering all the emotional labor."

Jamie using the phrase *emotional labor* impressed her; most men in their generation didn't believe such a thing existed, much less bother to understand how it affected the female half of the species. The modern world understood so much more about women and the roles they had been burdened with throughout history, but men her age...well, there was more than one reason she and Kirk had grown apart. To say her thinking had become more liberal as the years passed might be an understatement.

His warmth was seducing her as much as his words, and she couldn't allow that. "You're right; that does fit," she agreed, continuing up the sidewalk.

Jamie didn't protest, just fell in step beside her. They walked in silence another block. Finally he brought her to a stop with a gentle hand on her elbow. "Iris, you know there's nothing to worry about here."

"There's not?" There definitely was. There was too much to worry about—which was why she was desperate to escape.

"No."

He cupped her cheek, and she couldn't stop herself from nuzzling into the touch. She'd forgotten how good touch could feel. Her daughter and son hugged her, and the younger children at the library gave her the occasional kiss on the cheek or hug or held her hand with their sticky little fingers. But it wasn't the same as male-female contact. She'd missed it more than she'd realized.

Danger, danger, Will Robinson!

She stepped back from his touch. "Jamie, I—" She stopped, swallowed hard, then forced herself to make eye contact. "I'm not ready for this. I thought maybe I was"—*no, you just couldn't resist temptation*—"but I'm not. I'm so not." A deep breath steadied her, gave her the courage to tell him, "I don't think I'll ever be ready for this. I'm sorry."

Without waiting for a response, she hurried up the sidewalk, catching up to Scarlett and Claire at the next cross street. She didn't look at Jamie when he arrived at her side, or for the rest of the walk to the hotel. She avoided standing next to him in the elevator, and when they exited on their floor, she didn't look back to see if he followed, but follow he did. He said good night to Scarlett with a brief brush of his lips across her cheek—Iris fought a surge of jealousy at the innocent touch—then did the same with Claire before turning to her. Her friends withdrew hastily through the door.

Jamie held out his hand. "Iris."

She laid her hand in his, tried to ignore the warmth of his fingers surrounding hers. When his knuckles nudged under her chin to lift her face, she resisted.

"Just look at me, Iris. Please."

She couldn't ignore that husky request. Raising her eyes, she met the dark green of his. "Jamie—"

He placed a finger over her lips. "It's okay."

Was it? "So you understand?"

His smile was gentle. "Oh, I understand."

"And you're okay with that?"

He shook his head. "I'll never be okay with you walking away from me."

Her heart dropped into her stomach.

"But I'm a patient man." His smile took on a wolfish edge. "And I don't mind a pursuit."

Her brain froze, his words ringing in her ears. "What—"

But Jamie wasn't answering. Instead he dipped his head, brushed his lips across hers—not her cheek, as he had with the others, but her quivering mouth—and then he was stepping back, his fingers holding hers until the very last second. "Good night, Iris." He winked. "See you soon."

She watched him until he stopped in front of the elevator, then made a hasty exit into her room. Scarlett and Claire pinned her with their wide eyes as soon as she stepped inside.

"Wow!" Claire said.

"Wow indeed," Scarlett agreed. "What the hell was that kiss?"

"It was hot, that's what it was." Claire's grin was impish. "Made me wish my Lincoln was here instead of sleeping with you two."

"Hey!" Scarlett picked up a pillow off the bed and slung it at Claire, who ducked out of the way, giggling. Iris hoped they'd get caught up in their fun and forget the real topic of this conversation.

No such luck.

Claire pushed her dark curls away from her eyes. "So? What happened, Iris?"

"It was just a kiss, nothing more."

Scarlett didn't seem to be buying it. "Did he ask you out?"

She shouldn't be disappointed at the answer. *You don't want a relationship, remember?* "No." She didn't tell them she hadn't given him a chance. She couldn't. Maybe they would understand—Claire had been divorced, she knew, though Scarlett had not. Still, they would likely understand—and try to talk her out of how she was feeling. She didn't need that right now. What she needed was a good night's sleep and to put this behind her.

And pray she could forget the feel of Jamie's mouth on hers, his body against hers, sooner rather than later. She was very afraid, though, that she would be revisiting those moments as soon as she closed her eyes.

Seven

Iris entered the back room of the library and sighed in contentment. As much as she enjoyed working with the public, especially the kids, she loved this room the most —the place where books were piled high, waiting to be sorted, labeled, and shelved; where the smell of old paper and new covers permeated the air; where quiet reigned and she could get lost in the thousands of worlds just waiting to be discovered.

But not without interruption.

"Iris!"

She turned from the stack of boxes containing the new purchases for the month. "Yes?"

Jennifer pushed her long hair back from her face, a harried expression in her eyes. "Mr. Shelton refuses to let me check him out. He's holding up the line."

Iris couldn't help but smile. She suspected the dementia Harry Shelton was experiencing was getting worse, but the man still loved his books. His daughter brought him to the library every Thursday for a new load, although lately he'd been picking up the same books over and over, as if the famil- iarity comforted his mind in the midst of the chaos he must be experiencing. Routine helped as well, which was why only Iris was allowed to check out his books. She'd been at the library as long as he'd been coming, and her face seemed to be the only one he could remember from the staff here. She was pleased she was able to provide that small bit of stability for him.

She turned her back on the new books with a pang of regret and returned to the checkout counter. "Harry, how are you doing today?"

The tension in Harry's age-bowed shoulders relaxed as he focused in on her. "Iris."

She extended her hand for his stack of books. "What treasures did you find?"

Once she was at the checkout desk, it usually took an hour minimum before she could get away again. Today was no different. Luckily a lull right before noon allowed her to escape back to the new arrivals.

She'd barely unpacked the first box before the door swung open and her daughter walked through. Iris held back a sigh.

"Krista! I didn't expect you today."

Her daughter's smile, so like Iris's, lit up her face. She reminded Iris of herself back when she was fresh out of college, about to marry Kirk, with her whole life ahead of her. Krista held up the take-out boxes in her hand. "I took a half day for a dentist appointment, so I brought you lunch."

Iris's stomach growled. "Patty's?" she asked hopefully. Patty's Deli was just off the square, known around town as the home of the best baked meatball subs. Iris preferred her Philly steak and cheese, and a quick sniff told her that was precisely what Krista had brought her.

Krista's smile had turned into a frown, and Iris frowned back. "What?"

Krista shook her head, though the frown was still present, and nudged the boxes in the direction of the door behind Iris that led to the break room. "Got time to eat?"

After checking to be certain Jennifer had everything under control for a bit, Iris led the way to the back room. As they made themselves comfortable at the table, Iris couldn't help noting her daughter's disquiet. Opening the lid of her sandwich box, she inhaled the beautiful aroma of grilled meat and veggies. "What's going on, hon?"

Krista paid close attention to the dressing she was stirring into her side salad. When she didn't speak, Iris's stomach clenched. "What's wrong?"

Her question was much more urgent this time. Krista hesitated for a long moment and then, seeming to come to a decision, set her fork down and focused on Iris. Her lips pursed in that way she'd had since she was a preteen, the way that warned Iris she wasn't going to like whatever was coming. "Mom, what did you do to your hair?"

Startled, Iris fingered the short strands at the back of her neck. "What do you mean?"

"Your hair." Actual tears gathered in Krista's eyes. "I knew you were going to that spa in Nashville, but I had no idea you'd actually cut off all your beautiful hair."

"You don't like it?" Iris had been getting used to the new cut all week, but frankly, she loved it. The short style made her feel free in a way her heavy hair had not. It was as if cutting her long hair had allowed her to let go of some emotional attachment that had nothing to do with her looks and everything to do with her past. And it felt good.

"Honestly, no, I don't like it."

If she'd been slapped, Iris wouldn't have been more shocked.

Krista immediately reached for her hand where it lay on the table. "Don't look like that. I'm sorry." She shook her head. "It's just...such a surprise." She said the last word as if biting into a bitter lemon. "It's so, I don't know, not you."

"I think it's very much me. The new me."

Krista straightened, returning her attention to her food. "What was wrong with the old you?"

"Apparently a lot if your father is to be believed."

Now it was Krista's turn to be shocked. At first Iris had gone to great lengths not to speak ill of Kirk in front of the kids, but over time she realized they were adults. It wasn't up to her to safeguard their rose-colored glasses where their father was concerned. Kirk's decisions came with consequences, and part of that was their children seeing him as he truly was. So she'd begun to speak openly—if usually more obliquely than today—about their marriage and its end. Adam had, during one long conversation where he'd flat-out asked what had happened between them, actually thanked her for telling him the truth. Krista hadn't come to that point yet. In fact, she hadn't asked questions about the divorce other than what Iris had shared on her own.

A tear streaked down Krista's cheek, and Iris's heart squeezed. "Mom, there is nothing wrong with you."

"I know that, hon." She patted Krista's hand, wishing she could take her daughter's pain away. Krista had struggled more with the divorce than Iris had expected, but they all had to deal with the change. Kirk had left them no other choice. "I just wanted something fresh, new. And I like the way it turned out." She flipped the ends of her hair. "Kinda flirty, isn't it?"

Her playfulness seemed lost on her daughter. "It's such a waste. It will take years to grow it back out."

Iris didn't plan to grow it back out, but maybe that was a discussion for another day. She took a big bite of her sandwich. "Mmm, this is so good. Patty is the best."

After a moment's hesitation, Krista dug into her meatball sub. To Iris's relief, talk turned to more neutral topics. Iris knew she would likely take out the hurt that Krista's remarks had caused later, examine it, and deal with it in her own way, but for now she focused on spending time with her daughter instead.

"Adam called yesterday. He and Chloe are planning to fly in for July Fourth weekend," she said later.

Iris suspected that her son and his girlfriend were getting close to an engagement, or at least she hoped so. Chloe seemed to be good for him. He'd been happy moving to Seattle and settling into a new life, but that happiness had turned to true contentment once he found Chloe. A wisp of sadness caught at the edges of her attention, but she pushed it away. She wouldn't regret her marriage, at least not the early years. They'd given her two beautiful children, after all, and a lot of good memories, no matter how much the bad of recent years had tried to overshadow them.

"Maybe we could go to the lake?" Krista suggested.

"That would be fun."

Krista finished her sub and salad as she daydreamed about what they could do together at Douglas Lake. They'd spent many a day there when the kids were younger, but since Adam had moved and Krista had been in college, they hadn't had many outings as a family. It would be nice to have the day together, building new memories that centered around the three of them, getting used to not having Kirk with them. Having Adam here took the sting out of that thought. There was very little she enjoyed more than having her children around her, and a day at the lake sounded perfect.

"I was thinking you could come over tonight and we could have dinner, maybe watch a movie and do manicures. What do you think?"

Iris pulled her thoughts away from the upcoming holiday. "I wish I could, hon, but I'm meeting the girls at the Drunken Otter tonight."

Krista's scowl said she wasn't happy with that answer. Truth be told, she didn't seem to be happy with much lately.

Iris wished the divorce hadn't soured so much of Krista's joy. It was almost as if her daughter had reverted to being a teenager, clinging to her mom when she should be focused on spreading her wings. Anytime Iris told her no or did something she wasn't a hundred percent in favor of—like cutting her hair—Iris heard about it.

"Why do you like going there? Isn't it loud? Crowded?"

Iris held back a sigh. It felt like she'd sighed a lot in the past half hour. "You'd know if you would come with me." She'd invited Krista many times. "It's fun. Wings and drinks and dancing. Letting loose." She raised her brows at her daughter. "You'd enjoy it. And you'd like Scarlett and Lily and the others if you would give them a chance."

Krista had seemed to like Scarlett at first, but since the divorce, she'd refused any and all invitations to be with Iris's friends, almost as if she saw them as a bad influence. Today was no different. "No, thanks." Krista began gathering her lunch, letting Iris know she was done. "I've got to work tomorrow."

"So do I," Iris reminded her gently. "It's not like we get rip-roaring drunk and dance on the tables."

A jolt went through Krista's body. "I certainly hope not!"

Iris stood, following Krista to the trash can to throw away their boxes. She put an arm around her daughter and hugged her close. "You're too young to be this judgmental." She hoped her teasing tone allowed the comment to slip under her daughter's guard. It was the truth, but not a truth Krista would take too kindly to hearing.

"Mom!"

Iris laughed off the moment, and it wasn't until Krista had left that she turned her thoughts back to her daughter's comments. If only Krista knew—Iris had done much more risky things than going to the Drunken Otter on girls' night for a drink and dancing. She'd actually kissed a man! Krista would probably faint from the shock of knowing her mother had been so bold. Thoughts of Jamie had been frequent this week, but she tried to turn her attention away whenever possible. No matter how good the kiss had been, no matter how much she'd like talking to him, she didn't want to get involved with anyone. She couldn't handle another disaster, and falling in love, risking another man walking away from her, was certainly that.

No, thank you.

Eight

Ladies' night. He hadn't been to a ladies' night in a long time. He chuckled at the thought as he pulled on his dress shirt and buttoned the front down his chest. Sleeves rolled up. What was it his son had said women called that now? Arm porn? He flexed his forearm and noticed the muscles popping under his tanned skin. A redhead usually didn't tan, but he spent so much time outside with the horses that his skin hadn't had a choice. At least it looked good against the white of his shirt.

Would Iris notice? That's all he really cared about. He'd offer her *arm porn* all night if it would get her to notice him.

It had been five days and Baby was still holding on to her foal, so he slipped his cell into his pocket after making sure the vibrate function was on. He didn't want to risk missing contact if the music was too loud for him to hear. They were literally in the "any day now" period. Michael, his son, would be home this evening and keeping an eye on things while Jamie was out. He typically spent afternoons and evenings at the restaurant, but his assistant manager, Francisco, had the dinner shift covered tonight so he could be off, and Michael was watching things here as usual. All Jamie had to worry about was getting himself into town and finding a way to approach Iris so that it didn't appear that he was stalking her.

Which he wasn't, not really. At least not in a creepy way. He probably wouldn't know so much of her routine were it not for his friendship with Erin.

"Headed out?" Michael asked as Jamie passed through the kitchen. His dark auburn head was stuck inside the fridge, where he was rummaging around.

"I am." Jamie shoved his keys and wallet into the pocket of his dress slacks. "Are you stealing my food again?"

Michael had a kitchen in the bunkhouse they'd converted into an apartment for him to live in, not a hundred yards from Jamie's door, but his son preferred to eat here for some reason. Not that Jamie minded. It was nice to have Michael around. With Marilyn and the other hands, things were hardly ever silent, and Jamie found his occasional night off far too quiet when no one was coming in and out of his kitchen door.

Michael backed out of the fridge, a packet of ham caught between his teeth, arms piled high with sandwich fixings. "Forgot to get groceries," he mumbled, walking the food toward the kitchen island.

Jamie smirked. "Of course you did."

"Want one?" his son asked, spreading the bounty out on the counter.

"I've got wings waiting for me."

"Damn." Michale paused in his sandwich making. "That does sound good. Maybe—"

Jamie headed for the door. "No! I've got things to do that don't involve my son—and you've got a mare to keep an eye on."

"Sounds like I'm not the only one keeping my eye on a mare," Michael shot back, his grin sly.

"I'm not comparing a woman to a horse." Stopping with the door half-open, he turned back to his son and winked. "But I might introduce you if things go well."

Michael laughed, the sound reminding Jamie of the gruff rumble that usually came out of his own mouth. When had his child become a man? Many years ago, as Jamie knew full well, but sometimes he forgot that this wasn't his teenager anymore.

"Get after it, Dad," Michael called as Jamie walked out the door.

"I will!" He shook his head at his son's antics, but both his laugh and his footsteps were light as he made his way to the car.

The Drunken Otter was a favorite in Black Wolf's Bluff. Not only was it the only pub/bar in town (aside from a biker bar on the outskirts that most people wouldn't venture to), but Clayton Harding was known for the best wings money could buy. His golden sauce with its brown-sugar base was renowned throughout the state, the jars selling for around ten dollars a pop, though Jamie was pretty certain he could charge fifteen and still have trouble keeping them in stock. Ladies' night was especially popular. Jamie parked halfway up the street leading off the west side of the square, near the post office. Walking the block and a half back to the Drunken Otter didn't bother him; it was a mild summer night, a coolish breeze stirring the air and rustling through the tree leaves as he traveled beneath them. The closer he got to the south end of the square, the more foot traffic picked up, people going in and out of the pub, hanging around in clusters outside, strolling the square as they window-shopped the various stores. Jamie had come from a bigger town in Texas nearly thirty years ago, and yet he never got over the uniqueness of living in small-town Tennessee. It felt like home, even to those who had not been born here. As much as he enjoyed the occasional foray to Nashville or even New

York, he didn't think he'd ever want to leave this area permanently.

The crowd inside the Drunken Otter created a dull roar of sound that met Jamie at the door. Glancing around, he noticed several people he recognized, either from the restaurant or from other businesses, including Dr. Everest, who was sipping a beer at the bar with a gentleman he didn't recognize. At least he would know where to find her if Michael notified him that Baby had gone into labor. He smirked at the knowledge and continued to peruse the room until his gaze landed on the group he knew would contain the woman he was searching for.

Iris.

She stood amid several women, a cocktail in her hand and a gorgeous smile on her face. He couldn't get over the new cut of her hair. He'd loved it before, but this new style gave her an edge that he definitely thought suited her. Plus it made him want to run his fingers through it, fist the short strands at the back of her head, and hold her still for his kiss—and more.

Don't get ahead of yourself, old man.

He shook the thought of Iris in his bed off before it had unintended consequences that would be visible to anyone who looked his way, and headed for the bar to grab a drink, hoping Iris would see him before he approached her. No need to feed into the stalker vibe, right?

"Jamie!" Clay swung a white towel over his shoulder before extending a hand across the bar. "How's the business treatin' ya?"

Since they were in the same business, Clayton and Jamie often had plenty to talk about despite the difference in their ages. If Jamie had to guess, he'd say Clay was a good fifteen years younger than his fifty-eight. He shook the man's hand. "Grateful for a night off."

"You haven't been in here on a weeknight in a few years."

Clay gave him a sly grin as he pushed a glass below one of the beer taps. "Must be a reason for that."

Jamie held back a groan, not that his friend was likely to hear it over the noise. Small towns and their nosy ways. In Black Wolf's Bluff, everyone knew everyone else's business. He'd rather avoid that—more for Iris's sake than his own—so he shrugged as nonchalantly as he could manage. "Needed a change of pace—and some wings."

Clay grinned. "Uh-huh." He slid the pint glass he'd filled across the bar to Jamie. "Right."

Jamie refrained from rolling his eyes. "Just get me some of that special sauce and keep your mouth shut."

The grin got wider. "Sure thing, boss." Calling his order out to a passing waitress took no more than a second. "Where ya sittin'?"

Jamie hesitated, glancing over his shoulder. Sure enough, Erin and Lily had caught sight of him and gestured him toward their table when he caught their eyes.

"Never mind," Clay said before Jamie could respond. "I gotcha." He nodded toward the group. "Have fun with whoever you're here to see."

He'd have to ask Clay to keep his observations to himself, but not right now. That would simply draw more attention from anyone who overheard their exchange. With a warning look at his friend that he hoped would suffice for the moment, he turned his back on the bar and braced himself for whatever greeting Iris decided to give him. As he started across the room, Iris's gaze swept the space, landed on him. Those gray beauties lit up at the sight of him before quickly dropping to the floor.

That was all he needed to know. Iris might be fighting the attraction they so obviously shared, but like he'd told her, he was a patient man. For now he would allow proximity to work its magic.

"Don't normally see you here on a weeknight," Erin called

as he neared their table. Because of course she did. His friends needed to stop commenting on his habits.

Jamie took a moment to shake Gavin Blackwood's hand before responding. The Scotsman had obviously finished whatever business he'd had in New York and quickly hurried back to be at Scarlett's side. Falling back on the excuse he'd used with Clay, he said, "I was in the mood for some wings."

Erin's wrinkled brow said she was skeptical. Gavin chuckled. "Don't think the lass'll swallow that one, Jamie."

"I'm obviously spending far too much time with the lot of you—you're getting a bit too familiar."

Gavin's eyes fairly twinkled. "A bit, yeah." He raised his beer. "But I commend ya for tryin'."

Jamie laughed. Bending down to brush a kiss along Erin's flushed cheek, he whispered, "I don't give up easily."

Erin met his gaze as he rose back up, her own amused. "Good."

Jamie extended the same greeting to Scarlett, then Lily. He nodded at Lily's assistant, Evan, and his—girlfriend? Fiancée? —Alana before turning eagerly toward Iris. Gray eyes reluctantly met his green.

Iris cleared her throat. "Jamie."

"Iris." Her name on his lips held a wealth of meaning he couldn't hold back, though he tried for her sake. "You look amazing."

She was wearing a silky navy-blue top, his favorite color, especially now that he saw the way it complemented her fair complexion. White slacks hugged her gorgeous legs. She was average height for a woman, but the slight heels she wore made him think she would fit perfectly against him despite the extra inches he held on her. Bring her lips closer to his when she was in his arms. And he definitely wanted her in his arms.

Faint pink color flushed Iris's cheeks, but maybe that was

the influence of the drink in her hand. He didn't think so with the way the words, "T-thank you," stuttered off her lips.

It would take a few minutes for the food to arrive, and wouldn't you know it, a slow song was just starting on the jukebox. He extended his hand to her. "May I have this dance?"

Nine

Iris had felt the air change the minute she caught sight of him. For the briefest second, tears burned at the backs of her eyes—she didn't want to be this aware of him. Didn't want whatever this was happening between them to keep happening. And yet she couldn't deny that it was.

And she had a feeling Jamie wouldn't let her deny it, even if she could. The man was persistent, she'd give him that.

Blinking back the emotion, she kept a side-eye on him as she attempted to carry on with her conversation. If Scarlett's smirk was anything to go by, she wasn't doing a very good job. But really, Jamie would make anyone stutter. The sight of that hard, wide chest in his white dress shirt, the sleeves rolled up his sexy forearms, was enough to distract every woman in the room.

Scarlett leaned in. "Arm porn, amiright?"

Lord, was she. Jamie worked hard, that much was obvious, and his arms showed the evidence of just how hard. She could imagine him holding Baby's lead, keeping her in check, his forearms tight as he mastered the mare.

What she really wanted was for him to master her.

The thought sent a jolt of panic through her.

"Hey, you okay?" Scarlett asked, ever attuned to Iris's state of being. She was grateful for such an attentive friend at any other time, but right now? She really didn't want to talk about the thoughts roiling around in her head.

"Sure."

Scarlett frowned. Guess she hadn't hidden her true thoughts as well as she'd hoped. She laid a hand on her friend's arm. "I'll be fine, Scarlett. Promise."

"You better be," her friend muttered before turning as Jamie joined their group.

Greetings went all the way around until finally, Jamie came to her. Trying hard to ignore the avid gazes of what felt like every pair of eyes in the pub, she met that forest-green, all-too-knowing gaze. "Jamie."

"Iris." He swept a look down her body, and her nipples tightened. "You look amazing."

Damn her tendency to blush, even at her age. She'd done it more around Jamie than she had with anyone in years, a fact that made her even more self-conscious. "T-thank you."

That slight stutter drew forth his wicked grin. Iris felt that look all the way to her core.

Jamie extended his hand. "May I have this dance?"

She should say no. Being this close to him was tempting enough; being in his arms? Resistance at that point would be futile.

"That sounds great," Scarlett was saying next to her, the big traitor. She had ahold of Gavin's hand, and grabbed Scarlett with the other. "Come on!"

She had a feeling Jamie knew exactly what her friend was doing—the amusement lighting his eyes told her that much. Without making a big scene, she couldn't say no. With Scarlett's help, he had her exactly where he wanted her.

Exactly where she wanted to be.

Surrendering to the inevitable, she followed Scarlett and Gavin out to the dance floor, intensely aware of Jamie close behind her. Anticipation began a slow fizz in her belly. When Scarlett released her to move into Gavin's arms, Iris turned slowly toward her partner.

Jamie didn't hesitate. He scooped her against him, chest to breasts, those strong arms encircling her in a cage that, if she was truly honest with herself, she didn't want to escape.

Some of her conflict must have shown on her face, because Jamie bent to whisper in her ear, "Am I really that horrible a dancer?"

They'd just begun, so he had to know better. But Iris forced herself to relax against him. It was just a dance, after all, not the gallows.

She tipped her face up to meet his eyes. "You know you're not." In fact, even with her initial tension, he guided her expertly around the floor, through the myriad of couples enjoying the slow music as well. She hadn't done much slow dancing—Kirk had never been comfortable dancing with her, although she'd heard tales that he'd been the envy of all the other guys in his fraternity at college because girls flocked to him, being one of the few that would actually dance at the frat parties. Jamie didn't feel uncomfortable or stiff; he felt warm, his heat seeping into her, relaxing her muscles, focusing her attention solely on him and the pleasure of being held by a partner who obviously relished having her in his arms.

If she'd thought resistance was futile before, now she knew for a fact, there was no resisting this man.

Jamie's frown caught her attention. "What was that thought?"

She huffed a reluctant laugh. "You have to stop doing that."

He leaned back, meeting her eyes more fully but also aligning their bellies in a way that had her feeling far too intimate in a crowded room. "Doing what?"

She cleared her throat. "Reading me."

Jamie's voice dropped into a deeper register. "I like reading you, Iris."

"Jamie—"

He gathered her closer, tipped his head down so that his mouth brushed her ear. "It's okay, Iris. There's no obligation here, no commitment. Just two people enjoying their time together. Let those worries go."

Her fingers tightened on his biceps without thought. "I can't. I'm too—"

When she didn't finish that sentence, he finished it for her. "Scared?"

"Yes!" The word was abrasive, a Brillo pad scraping across her vocal cords, but it had to be said. He needed to know.

"I understand. I remember that fear very well."

Surprise jerked through her. "When were you afraid?"

It was an insolent question—everyone had personal fears. But men rarely admitted to them.

"After my own divorce."

Now it was her turn to lean back, look up at him. "You were divorced?" He'd been single as long as she'd known him, though she was pretty certain she'd heard he had a son. She'd been so caught up in her own situation that she hadn't given his as much thought as she probably should have. "I'm sorry."

Jamie brought his hand up to cup her cheek, his thumb starting that stroking thing he did anytime he touched her. "I appreciate that, but there's nothing for you to feel sorry for."

That wasn't what she'd meant, but she let it go. She should let the whole thing go, but she couldn't keep silent. "May I ask...what happened?"

His eyes got a distant look in them. "Brenda wasn't ready to be a mother. When Michael came along..." He shrugged. "Let's just say it was better for us to be on our own. I let her go."

Had there been abuse? Was Michael okay? So many questions, and none of them should she ask.

He stroked her cheek again. "Look at that worry in your eyes. Don't worry about us, Iris. We were okay. But having a son meant I had to be a lot more careful about any other relationship I allowed into my life."

A much more valid fear than hers, some would say, although she didn't think fears required validation. Everyone's circumstances were individual to them.

"It's normal to be afraid," Jamie was saying. "It's a normal part of life. What matters isn't that you have them; it's how you react that matters."

Not letting those fears control you, he meant. And yet fear was a basic biological response to keep one safe. A warning to not do something that could result in harm. And letting herself get involved with this man could definitely harm her. If her husband of twenty-three years couldn't love her enough to stay with her, how could a man like Jamie commit to a relationship with her?

That was it, wasn't it? The kernel of her fear. That she was unlovable, unworthy. That risking her heart would never pay off because her ex-husband had been a douche bag. It wasn't logical, but her heart was trying to keep her safe.

Maybe what she needed was just to be honest.

"Jamie…"

He chuckled.

"What?"

Jamie shook his head. "Every time you say my name in that tone of voice, I'm reminded of my third-grade teacher. She told me every single day of that year exactly where I was going wrong. Her standards were impossibly high."

Were Iris's?

"It's okay, Iris," Jamie told her, probably in response to some emotion flashing across her face. She swore it didn't matter if she held words back; her face said all that needed to be said despite her restraint. "I don't mind a little reprimand now and then."

Something about the way he said *reprimand* had her thinking he meant something far different. Heat flashed in her cheeks.

"Anyway, you were saying...?"

What had she been saying? Ah...

The song they were dancing to chose that moment to fade into the ether. The jukebox clicked over to "Jessie's Girl."

Iris shook her head. "Can we table this discussion for now?"

She sounded like she was in a city council meeting, but this wasn't the time nor place she wanted to reveal things as personal as she needed to reveal. Jamie's gentle smile said he understood. "Of course we can. I'm not going anywhere."

That's what he says now.

And it was that voice that terrified her.

Jamie joined them at the table piled high with golden chicken wings and beer. Of course he sat next to her, a maneuver he seemed to have perfected from their first meal together. Or maybe it was just that her friends were all couples and she and Jamie were the odd ones out. She tried to ignore his body heat, his laughter, the sheer enjoyment he found in consuming the "finger-lickin' good" wings Clayton was famous for, but there was no ignoring Jamie, she was coming to find. He was larger than life, and his presence drew her like a lodestone anytime he was in her vicinity. For tonight, she decided to relax and enjoy it.

Which was exactly what she did until the last wing was consumed. Her friends were a good antidote to whatever worried her, and she reveled in the joy of being with a group of people who truly cared about one another. That joy took a sharp nosedive when she glanced over to see Kirk and his fiancée walking through the door to the Drunken Otter.

Every muscle in her body froze, including the ones

holding the smile to her face. She hadn't seen Kirk since the engagement. She didn't want to see him now, but living in a small town meant it was inevitable, really. That didn't mean she wanted to stay.

A warm hand on her arm drew her attention away from the couple crossing to the bar.

Jamie.

"You okay?" he asked quietly.

She flashed him a weak smile, not wanting to meet his eyes. "Of course." She reached for her purse, hanging from the back of her chair.

"You're not leaving?" Scarlett exclaimed.

Iris shot a glance at the bar, then back to her friend. "I think I'll call it a night. But you stay." Scarlett and Gavin had picked her up, but she didn't want to ruin her friend's night. "I can call an Uber." There were usually drivers hanging around on Thursday nights, given the pub's popularity.

Scarlett was staring daggers at Kirk and Emmie. Iris didn't turn to look. She didn't care if he had that satisfied smirk on his face. What she cared about was protecting herself right now, and that meant not being in the same room with them.

Jamie stood beside her. "I'll take you home."

"No, no..."

Jamie leaned down, putting his face close to hers. The warm scent of beer and brown sugar brushed her face. "No arguing. You're not putting me out." He cupped her cheek like he had on the dance floor, his thumb stroking her cheekbone. "It will be my privilege."

How did she believe words like that? And yet, staring into his eyes, she knew they were true.

Goodbyes rang out from the rest of the group, and Iris acquiesced. She could feel a hot stare on her back as Jamie led her out of the pub, but she didn't look in Kirk's direction. She focused on moving forward. Her ex would not get the satisfaction of holding her back.

Ten

The light scent of Iris's perfume filled Jamie's nostrils as he handed her into the car. The intimacy of it tightened his groin. Something about being in a dark car with a woman filled a man with temptation. Maybe it was a throwback to those teen nights when parking was forbidden—not that he anticipated parking with Iris. He definitely wouldn't mind, but...

He closed her door firmly and rounded the back of his Mercedes. *Keep it together, old man.*

The warm purr of the engine filled the silence as he buckled his seat belt, then checked to be certain Iris had hers secure. Just as he put the car in reverse, his phone buzzed in his pocket. He pulled his cell out.

Michael.

"I need to take this, Iris. Just a sec."

Her soft smile stuck in his mind as he answered his son's call.

"Michael?"

"It's time, Dad."

Jamie swore his heart skipped a beat. "You're sure?"

His son chuckled in his ear. "How many times have we gone through this? I know what I'm talking about."

"Of course you do." Michael helped him manage the herd; if he said Baby was in labor, she was in labor.

"I'm calling Dr. Everest as soon as I get off the phone with you."

Since she was still at the pub, she would be right behind him. Except he had Iris to take care of.

"All right. I'll be there asap."

Michael hung up without answering. Jamie turned toward Iris. "Baby is in labor."

Her eyes went wide, a brilliant smile lighting her face. "Finally!"

Yes, finally. Anticipation thrummed in his belly alongside nerves.

Iris was reaching for the door handle. "I can get a ride—"

He didn't know where the impulse came from, but he gripped her wrist, holding her in the car. "Come with me."

Iris shook her head. "What?"

Yes, this felt right. "Come with me." He smiled, letting his excitement free. "Have you ever seen a foal born?"

Iris settled back in her seat. "No, but—"

"Then come with me." Honestly, he couldn't think of anyone he wanted to share this moment with more than the woman beside him. "Iris, I can take you home, no worries. We have time. But…come with me. Please."

The words to convince her were on his lips, but he held them back. She already knew how important Baby was to him. She knew how much he had worried and waited for this moment. And she wanted to come; he could see it in her eyes. All she had to do was overcome her hesitation enough to say yes.

The tension that seemed ever present in her body when she was with him slowly relaxed. "Yes. I'd love to—"

Go with you? See the miracle of life being brought into the world? *Spend more time with you*? He wasn't certain how she'd planned to finish that sentence, and he found right now he didn't care. All that mattered was the word *yes*. He couldn't hold himself back—he surged in to kiss her hard on the mouth. Before she could respond, he was back behind the wheel. "Let's go. I promise I'll take you home after."

From the corner of his eye he saw Iris reach up to touch her lips, and satisfaction filled his chest.

"How long does labor normally last?" Iris asked as he pulled away from the curb.

"A few hours, though it varies just like with women. But Baby usually delivers pretty quickly."

"Lucky girl," Iris muttered. He gathered that meant her own labors had not been short. Sympathy tugged at him, remembering Michael's delivery and how long it had taken to bring him into the world, how hard it had been to watch another human being suffer like that, and he grasped her hand where it lay on the console between them. She jerked at his touch, but she didn't pull away. They traveled in companionable silence, her hand inside his, for several minutes before he reached the turnoff to the interstate.

"How far out of town do you live?" Iris asked.

"About halfway between Black Wolf's Bluff and Gatlinburg. My place is situated on the northern end of Douglas Lake." He'd been lucky to discover the land before buying in the area had become too precious to afford.

They absently talked about the lake and the ranch until Jamie reached the gate at the head of his driveway, marked prominently with a wrought-iron carousel horse with the words *Flying Horse Ranch* encircling it. He reluctantly released Iris's hand to signal the remote. As he pulled through, a truck moved into the driveway behind his car—Dr. Everest. He waited for her to pass the gate before signaling it to close. The two vehicles reached the house just as Michael jogged up from the path to the barn.

"My son," Jamie told Iris, a hint of pride in his voice. Iris's look said she heard it and understood. They exited the car at the same time.

Michael was breathing heavy as he met them at the front of the car. "I think something's wrong."

"What?" Laura called as she slammed her truck door closed. Without pause she hurried to the back to grab her equipment.

Jamie listened, fear rising, as Michael described what was going on. Normally Baby's labor progressed within a couple of hours, but Michael had been watching her for almost that long, and other than restlessly lying down and getting up repeatedly, she did not appear to be advancing. Excessive sweating, restlessness, obvious distress.

"Any sign of the foal?" Jamie asked.

"No presentation, and her water hasn't broken, but no red bag," Michael confirmed.

Iris made a small sound as if confused. "It's a sign of premature placental abruption," Jamie explained. He hadn't realized his hands were fisted at his sides until Iris gathered one between hers, her gentle strokes along his forearm and the back of his hand expressing compassion without words.

Laura joined them, equipment in hand. "Let's go."

Michael tossed a set of keys to Jamie, taking a second pair in his hand. They jogged toward the ATVs at the head of the lane down to the barn. Jamie glanced back at Iris, sudden concern hitting him. Taking in her white pants and heels, he said, "You're not really dressed for this."

"You've got time," Laura yelled over her shoulder as she hopped onto Michael's ATV. "I need to examine her and get the lay of the land."

Torn between taking care of his two girls, Jamie hesitated.

"It's okay, Jamie. I'll be fine."

But Iris wouldn't be fine, not if Baby required longer than expected to deliver. Taking a firm hold on his emotions, he turned back and took her elbow, guiding her toward the house. "We have a few minutes. Let's get you taken care of."

The trip through the house was a blur. He hoped at some point that Iris became intimately familiar with his home—especially his bedroom—but right now wasn't the time. He led her into the primary at the far end of the house, crossed to the night stand, and flipped on a lamp. He'd always hated overhead lights shining in his eyes, and his room was set up mostly with lamplight. Moving toward the closet, he threw over his shoulder, "Let me grab you something to change into."

Iris was sputtering excuses behind him, but he ignored her. As he rummaged through his dresser, he found some thin cotton sweatpants and a T-shirt that, while they would definitely be big on her, would work for the time being. He carried them over to her. "Trust me?"

A tiny smile played over her lips despite the concern in her eyes. "Of course I do."

He handed her the clothes. "You don't want to get your clothes dirty in the barn. I should've thought of that before inviting you, but…"

Iris stared intently up at him. "But what?"

"But I wanted you here too much to think about anything else."

Her face softened, and for the very first time, she reached for him instead of the other way around. Her warm hand landed on his chest, pressed firmly against his heart. "I don't know what to say."

"Don't say anything." Though he wanted to keep her touching him forever, he urged her toward the en suite. "Just change so I know you'll be more comfortable while we wait."

While Iris was in the bathroom, he grabbed some jeans and a shirt and changed in the walk-in closet, then retrieved a couple pairs of sports socks from his top drawer. The bathroom door opened a minute after he returned to the bedroom

—obviously Iris wasn't one to make a fuss about wearing his clothes. Although he had to say, seeing his favorite T-shirt on her did funny things to his gut. He handed over a pair of socks. "I think Marilyn, my housekeeper, has some rain boots in the mudroom that should fit you."

Iris looked over his change of clothes, her gaze appreciative, took the socks without complaint, and followed him back to the kitchen. When they'd both donned socks and boots, he led her out to the ATV. They were at the barn no more than ten minutes after Laura and Michael.

"What's happening?" he asked as Michael turned at his approach. His son stood at the half door to the birthing stall, one arm resting on top. The fluorescent lights above the generously spaced stall highlighted the copper tones of his hair and the unease darkening his eyes.

"Not sure yet." The words were tense—Michael held almost as much affection for Baby as Jamie did. Still his gaze swept behind Jamie toward Iris, and a tinge of amusement lightened his voice. "Your mare?" he asked under his breath.

Jamie gave Michael a warning look. Turning to Iris, he gathered her closer to him. "Iris, this is my son, Michael. Michael, this is Iris Daniels."

The two shook hands while Iris smiled warmly. "It's a pleasure to meet you, Michael. I only wish it were under less concerning circumstances."

"Thank you." Michael's words were sincere, as was the appreciation in his eyes.

The three of them turned when Laura approached.

"How is she, Doc?" Jamie asked.

The vet's brow was knitted—not a good sign. Jamie tensed.

"She's not showing signs of a rupture or abruption, but I'm not feeling the foal in the canal either."

"Is she breech?" Michael asked.

Laura shook her head. "I don't think so. The baby was in

position the last time I checked her." Looking back at Baby, who prowled the stall restlessly, she said, "Could be the foal is bigger than we thought. Not sure. Right now we will monitor, but if she doesn't progress soon…"

Jamie felt a lump in his throat, and his hand tightened in Iris's. Baby and the foal had to be all right. He couldn't accept anything less.

He spent the next hour in the stall, alternating between rubbing Baby's cheek as she pressed her forehead to his chest, and sitting beside her, crooning to her with long sweeps of his hand down her sweaty neck as she lay on her side. Minutes seemed to tick by like molasses, but every time he glanced up, Iris was right there at the stall door, her arms resting atop it, staring intently at him while he cared for the mare. Sometimes she spoke quietly with Michael or Laura, but most of the time she was silent, watching and waiting right along with him. He felt her presence as if she were standing or sitting beside him, felt the encouragement and support he needed so badly, and he realized in those long moments that he wanted this in his life—her at his side, and him at hers, supporting each other, encouraging each other. Loving one another.

Yes, love. Did he love her right now? They hadn't known each other long enough for that to happen, but he knew himself, and he knew this was different than any other relationship he'd ever considered or been involved in. He wanted this with every fiber of his being, and the thought of not having it, not having her… He couldn't consider that possibility any more than he could consider anything but a perfect outcome for Baby and her foal.

Baby was standing, her head at his chest, when he felt her push hard against him. A glance told him her muscles were tensing through her belly. "She's pushing."

Laura was at his side immediately. Her competent hands ran along Baby's stomach, and suddenly a gush of liquid escaped the mare, telling them Baby's water had broken. Laura waited, with Jamie barely breathing, until the constriction in Baby's muscles let up. A smile lightened the tension that had held them all frozen. "Yep. Looks like we're moving."

The next half an hour seemed to take a lifetime. Laura checked again, and though she found one hoof and the foal's nose in the birth canal, the second hoof was missing. It took some maneuvering, but she was finally able to correct the foal's position, and shortly thereafter, two small hooves appeared at the opening. Jamie felt like cheering but settled for crooning to Baby, who decided to lie down one final time. Every muscle in her body came to bear on her baby, and within minutes the filly was born.

The birth relieved both of them, he was sure, but especially his Baby. As her foal left her body, his mare gave the biggest sigh, the sound exhausted. A soft whinny left her closed muzzle.

"That's right. She's finally here, love," Jamie whispered to her.

But all wasn't over. As he watched, heart in his throat, Laura worked to get the foal breathing. Tense silence filled the stall, and when he glanced at Iris, he saw tears glistening on her cheeks, eyes glued to the tiny filly now lying in the straw. Moments later a cough sounded from the newborn, and when Laura backed away, the filly tossed her head in the air, looking for her mama.

Finally.

The relief nearly shattered him. Seeming unaware of the drama, Baby moved calmly to her feet, over to her foal, and began to clean the little one's sleek black coat. Jamie got to his feet as well and, after checking that the baby was definitively alert, made a beeline for Iris. Across the barrier of the door, her warm arms surrounded him, and only then did he feel like he could take a full breath for the first time in hours.

Eleven

Watching Jamie with Baby and her new foal felt like watching a father with his newborn child. It softened Iris's heart in a way she hadn't expected, and seeing him cuddle the spindly filly and help it stand to nurse melted her almost as much as all those "sexy daddy cuddling a newborn" images on the covers of romance novels. Her ovaries might have given up the ghost a couple of years ago—thank goodness for hereditary early menopause and not having periods till she was almost sixty—but it still felt like they exploded as she observed the aftermath of the birth from the door of the stall.

Michael seemed as involved as his father, though it was obvious Baby favored Jamie. It wasn't until a couple of hours after the birth, when Michael had escorted the vet to one of the ATVs to take her back to her truck, that Jamie came to the door and leaned against it. Her heart fluttered as he lifted one arm and gripped the post that served as a doorjamb above her head.

Arm porn indeed. He even had "the lean" down pat. So unfair.

"You look dead on your feet," he said, voice rough with use and emotion.

"Thanks," she murmured, a wry smile quirking up one side of her tired lips.

Jamie grinned, and though it was sexy, she had to admit he looked tired as well. The exhaustion of being Baby's birth coach looked good on him, though.

"You know what I mean."

She nodded. "I do. And I feel guilty having you take me home." Her fingers itched to smooth away the lines of fatigue feathering out from the corners of his eyes.

"It's not—a—big—" The word cut off with a deep yawn.

"It's not?" she asked. "I think it is."

He chuckled. Stepping back, he opened the door and joined her in the center aisle of the barn. "Okay, so the excitement of the night is hitting me. Doesn't mean I can't drive you home."

"Jamie, that's an hour round trip for you. I live on the other side of Black Wolf's Bluff. If I'd thought about it before we came out here, I would have called a ride hours ago." But she hadn't thought about it, and now it was the middle of the night. Did she dare wake Scarlett to come get her? Her friend worked from home, but she didn't want to presume that meant Scarlett could sleep in tomorrow and not be up early for work.

Jamie slid an arm around her waist, the feeling both foreign and somehow familiar, and turned her toward the open doors of the barn. "I have a proposal that might solve this dilemma."

"You do?" she asked warily. Surely he wasn't about to proposition her.

"My guest room is completely empty and available."

Did she dare? Something about the idea of spending the night in Jamie's house felt...odd. Maybe because she hadn't "spent the night" with a man other than Kirk, well, ever. But he wasn't inviting her into his bed. Fatigue pulled at her, urging her to accept, but...

Michael drove up as they arrived at their own ATV. Jamie handed Iris onto the vehicle, then turned back to his son. "You've got this covered?"

Michael gave his dad a much perkier grin than either she or Jamie could probably manage. "Of course. Got my nap in this afternoon just in case."

"Good. Call me if anything comes up, all right?"

"Will do." Michael winked at his dad. "Sleep well."

Iris was too tired to blush, but the urge was there. Instead she buried her face behind Jamie's back as he joined her on the ATV. Seconds later they were off and Michael's laughter was left behind.

"Don't mind him," Jamie said after turning off the ATV at the house. "He might tease, but he doesn't spread rumors."

She hated to admit a surge of relief filled her. She wasn't doing anything wrong, even if she did choose to have sex with Jamie, but the sense that she was wouldn't leave her. Was it because her mind still felt like she was cheating on Kirk, despite the fact that they were divorced? *And* despite the fact that she wasn't sleeping with Jamie?

Lord, if she was going to feel guilty, she should just do it. At least then she'd have something to feel guilty about.

Just the thought of having Jamie touch her, of seeing him naked, exploring him, enjoying him, had her hot and bothered no matter how tired she was. As he guided her off the ATV, the firm grip of his hand translated in so many ways—how he would grip her, guide her, how his touch might firm as he became more aroused. Was he dominant in bed, or did he prefer to sit back and let her do all the work, like Kirk had? She'd tried for years to encourage Kirk to take the lead, but after frustration had her lashing out in ways she hadn't liked, she'd decided to let it go and accept that she at least had an enjoyable sex life, if not the one she'd fantasized about. She'd been a virgin when she married Kirk, with virtually no experience, and felt she should at least be grateful that she experienced orgasm most of the time, unlike many of her friends through the years. Still, the idea that Jamie might be the kind of lover she'd always daydreamed about, the kind in the romance novels she loved to read between the "literature" and nonfiction she also devoured, had her mind racing ninety to nothing in the dim light of his home.

Jamie led her down the hall they'd used earlier tonight, stopping at a large closet to gather towels and washcloth. "You can shower in the morning if you like. Save you time when you get home." He opened the door on the opposite side of the hall from his bedroom. "Marylin keeps things stocked and fresh, so I know the linens have been washed and the bathroom will have anything you might need."

Thank goodness, because the idea of making a bed at this time of night had her wanting to whimper. She hated making beds. Seemed silly, but all that pulling and tugging and finagling drove her crazy. She'd never admit it to anyone else, but in the past few months she'd occasionally curled up with a blanket, the pile of freshly washed sheets next to her, left to be put in place the next day.

"I appreciate this, Jamie."

He set the towels on the neatly made bed, but Iris had little time to notice and appreciate the cream-colored comforter set with its hand-stitched embroidery before Jamie gathered her into his arms. It seemed completely natural to relax against him, to let his hard chest pillow her breasts, allow his firm arms to bring her close, aligning their bodies in ways that woke her up instead of the opposite. And then Jamie whispered hoarsely in her ear.

"Thank you for staying, Iris. It meant so much to me to have you here, to share this with you."

The rough emotion filling his voice left no doubt that he meant what he'd said. But why? Why did having *her* here mean so much? What drew this man to her? Why would he want her when she'd made it abundantly clear she wasn't ready, might never be ready to risk her heart again?

What if your heart wasn't at risk? You don't have to risk anything just for sex. To be held for one night. To not be alone for a little while.

She drew back the slightest bit, just enough to look Jamie in the eye. What she saw there had the heat inside her flaming higher. Without thought, she leaned in, wanting to taste the fire she read so clearly in his eyes.

His lips were warm, somehow familiar by now—and hard. Jamie didn't passively receive her kiss; no, he went after her tongue immediately, delving inside, tangling his tongue with hers as if he couldn't wait to taste her.

She responded without hesitation.

All thought, all concern left her as she surrendered to Jamie's touch. She knew now, without doubt, that his hands did indeed touch her dominantly when he was aroused. That his grip did become tighter. That he went after what he wanted with confidence, not a single hint of uncertainty. That he groaned when she slid her palms up the muscles that bordered his spine, and quivered when she reversed direction, stopping just shy of the firm globes of his rear.

God, she wanted her hands there. She didn't dare, but she did want. Her fingers itched to grip him and drag him closer.

She settled for splaying her hands in the small of his back, warming him even as the roaming of his hands warmed her. Her nipples tight when his fingers brushed close, his hands closing on her biceps, his fingertips just grazing the sides of her breasts. When she arched against him, her mouth opening on a gasp, he did it again. And again.

When he grazed the tips of her breasts, she couldn't help it —she went rigid, and not with desire. With shock.

What was she doing? Was she prepared to have sex with him? That one touch brought full awareness to her mind—the direction they were heading, the overwhelming desire to let it happen, and the realization of exactly what she would be opening herself up to if they did.

A relationship. With Jamie. Because despite what she might tell herself, she knew there was no way she could take this step and have it be anything but casual. She couldn't divorce herself from the man she was making love to; if she hadn't known that before, she knew it now without doubt. Could she accept that and walk away whole?

No.

Jamie must have felt the change in her body, because he paused. "Is this okay?"

His words...God, the sound of that rough need in his voice made her ache to keep going. But she couldn't. She wasn't ready. Unable to speak, she shook her head.

Jamie immediately lifted his hands away from her body, but he didn't let go. Instead, despite the urgent demand his body was making—that she was just now becoming aware of —he circled his arms around her and held her tightly against him, unmoving, as they both began the lengthy journey back to calm.

Finally, long minutes later, Jamie murmured into her hair, "Let me go get your things."

Iris regretted the loss of his warmth as he backed away. Maybe if she didn't have so many hang-ups... But no, she couldn't think that way. This was a journey, and not one anyone could undertake or understand for her. She hated hurting him, but she knew she had to make the decision that was best for herself. If the time was eventually right, it would happen, but not now, not like this, with uncertainty inside her. So she shut down the disappointment and waited for Jamie's return.

When he entered, he held her clothes in one hand and her purse in the other. She thanked him, taking the pile, but Jamie didn't let go. Her startled gaze shot up to his.

"Sleep well, Iris," he said, the words sounding like gravel in his throat. She'd done that, excited him, aroused him. A flash of pleasure filled her even as he leaned in, his lips brushing hers lightly before he made a hasty retreat to the hall and shut her door.

She stood there, stunned at the intensity of such a slight kiss, stunned at the change to her life that just a few minutes could make, before a buzzing coming from her purse drew her back to reality.

Her phone. She hadn't even realized she'd left it behind at the house. The entirety of her thoughts had been focused on Jamie and Baby and the newborn foal. Pulling the cell from her purse, she noted that the buzzing had been another in a long line of incoming texts from her daughter.

Damn.

KRISTA: Mom, where are you?!?!?!

A sigh left her. She knew her daughter well enough to know Krista wouldn't stop texting if Iris didn't respond, but Iris really didn't want to respond. She didn't want to talk. She wanted to lie down in the warm bed and think about nothing but Jamie. Not decisions. Not responsibility. Nothing but the warmth of the man who made her want to take risks she wasn't sure were good for her.

IRIS: I'm here. Forgot my phone was on silent in my purse. Will talk to you in the morning! [kissy face]

And then she turned off the phone. She told herself it was to save the battery, but it wasn't the truth. She'd face her daughter's wrath in the morning, but tonight was just for her. She climbed into bed and closed her mind to guilt as she drifted off to sleep, hoping Jamie would visit her dreams like he had so many times before.

Twelve

I ris muttered a curse word under her breath when she and Jamie pulled into her apartment complex not long after dawn the next morning.

"You okay?" Jamie asked.

"I was," she grumbled. And she had been. She'd gotten a few restful hours of sleep across the hall from Jamie last night, and woke early enough to take a quick shower before meeting him in the kitchen so he could drive her home. Things felt pleasant this morning, not awkward or embarrassing. Not like a morning after.

So why did she feel guilty seeing Krista knocking on her front door when they pulled into a space outside her apartment?

Jamie caught on quickly. He gave a low whistle. "Your daughter?"

"Yes." Iris sighed. *Please don't make a scene, Krista. Please.*

But that was wishful thinking at its finest. As they watched, Krista turned toward the car, saw her mother in the front seat, and after a moment or two of openmouthed gaping, began stomping down the stairs.

"Should we get out?" Jamie whispered dramatically in her

direction.

"Can we run away instead?"

He laughed, the sound deep-throated and not at all scared. And then he opened his door and got out.

Iris was thinking about hopping into the driver's seat and racing away. Unfortunately that would mean running over Jamie as he circled behind the car to come to her door, and he was too fine a man to flatten like a pancake, so instead she braced herself for confrontation.

You're an adult, remember? Even if it feels like you are facing an accusatory parent. When had their roles become reversed?

When she got a divorce, of course. Maybe Krista didn't believe she could take care of herself because she'd only seen Iris as part of a couple, not paying attention to the fact that Iris handled everything in their lives mostly on her own, as most women did. She was fully capable, but somehow Krista had missed that memo and chose to treat her like a child instead. Iris simply hadn't had the courage to call her on it yet, hoping time would allow Krista to move on without the need for confrontation.

Looked like that time was up.

Jamie opened Iris's door just as Krista arrived on the sidewalk in front of his car.

"Mom!"

At the harsh tone, Iris shot her daughter a sharp look. "Don't yell at me, Krista."

"Y-you— You—" She gestured at Jamie, at the car, at Iris's clothes that obviously weren't for work. "You want to get on to me about yelling when you've been…you've been…"

Iris's body went stiff with shock and not a little fear of what would leave her daughter's mouth next. "Krista!"

Jamie stood next to her, his body blocking her from moving out of the vee of the car and the door that cradled her. She felt more than saw him go stiff, and a sick feeling shot through her. He'd never met Krista before, and Iris hated that this was the way that would happen, but it would be even worse if Jamie stepped in to put Krista in her place. Likely Krista would never forgive him.

Or Iris.

She didn't stop to examine why that mattered. Thank goodness he stayed quiet, though he did place a warm hand of support at the base of her spine and step back, giving her room to fully exit the car.

Krista wasn't finished. "What am I supposed to think? You come home at the crack of dawn with some strange man after a night out—obviously all night—and expect me to, what, just ignore it? I was terrified, Mom. You wouldn't answer your phone; you didn't answer your door this morning. I worried myself sick, and you were off, what, hooking up with some guy?"

That Jamie didn't let pass. "Stop," he said, his voice quiet but firm with authority. Krista instinctively stiffened, but her mouth clamped shut nonetheless.

Just like always. Why did kids listen to that deep voice when it was their mother who tried to train most of the good sense into them?

Iris squared her shoulders, ignoring her embarrassment at Krista's words, the disappointment that her daughter would even think of speaking to her like this. She couldn't allow Jamie to fight her battles for her. "Whatever happened between Jamie and me is none of your business, Krista," she said, mimicking Jamie's firm tone. She walked toward the stairs, bypassing her daughter. "He's a friend who gave me a ride home, and you are repaying his kindness with insults and bad behavior." She took the first stairstep, then the next, making her way toward her apartment on the second floor. "I'm sorry I didn't answer this morning, but I responded last night to let you know I was fine. That should be enough."

Iris could hear Jamie on the steps behind her, feel his heat at her back. Whether Krista followed, she wasn't sure, not until she reached her front door and turned to thank Jamie. "I appreciate you bringing me home."

Krista glared behind Jamie's back, but he ignored her daughter's presence. "Thank you for going with me last night." He gave her a slight smile, letting his hand glide down her arm in a comforting gesture hidden from Krista by his body. "I'll call you later. Have a good day at work."

Iris was at once disappointed that he left without a goodbye kiss, and forever grateful that he didn't add fuel to Krista's fire. She and her daughter waited silently on the landing until Jamie had started his car and pulled out of the parking lot. Only then did Iris allow exactly how she felt about Krista's behavior out into the open. "You should be ashamed of yourself."

Harsh words, but they were true. Hurt flashed in Krista's eyes, but Iris refused to soften the blow. She unlocked her door and walked inside.

Krista followed.

In the apartment's tiny kitchen, Iris collected a glass, went to the refrigerator, and poured some juice, just for something to do with her hands. She needed to get ready for work, but she didn't want Krista following her into the bathroom to do her makeup and cornering her there. She also didn't know what more to say. On some level she understood that her daughter was regressing, and it was somewhat to be expected during a major event like a divorce. But Krista was twenty-one. Even had *she* come home with a man early in the morning, Iris might have confronted her, but not like that. Krista had practically called her a whore. That blow hurt more than she wanted to admit out loud.

"Mom—"

Iris set her glass down on the counter, planted her hands on the cool granite, and stared at her daughter, waiting for another strike to come. Krista took one look at her and clamped her mouth shut.

Iris pulled in a deep breath, searching for calm. Only when she felt she had a firm handle on her emotions did she allow herself to speak. "Krista, I get that you have struggled with the divorce. I've tried to be patient. But I am not a teenager, nor am I your child. You don't get to police my life, which may or may not—*eventually*—include a man." She would have used the word *never* before she met Jamie, but then… "But Jamie is just a friend."

That mutinous look returned to her daughter's eyes. "I saw the way he looked at you, Mom." She squared off on the other side of the counter and smacked her hands down, mimicking Iris's stance. "He had his hand on your lower back. No 'friend' touches someone that way. He might tell you he wants to be your friend, but he's angling for something else."

"So?" Exasperation had her fighting the urge to round the counter and shake some sense into Krista. "Why is it bad if he looks at me in a more than friendly way? I am a woman. A single woman at that. Your father is already engaged to someone else, and I don't hear you ranting about him."

"That's different. He's—"

"How is it different, Krista?" She paused, forcing herself to gentle her voice, to guide instead of demand. "Are there different standards for men than women?" She hadn't raised Krista that way—men and women were equal, if not exactly the same, in accomplishments and expectations. This teenage obsession had to stop.

"You're my mom."

"I may be your mom, but I am also me, with my own life to live and my own decisions to make. Those decisions are not yours; they're mine."

"But…" Her daughter's eyes filled with tears. The sight wiped away Iris's lingering anger.

"Krista." She rounded the corner and gathered her daughter into her arms. "It's going to be okay. I know this transition hasn't been easy for any of us, but it's going to be okay."

"But what if you find someone else and leave me behind."

Iris's heart broke. Was that how Krista felt about Kirk's new relationship, that it was taking her place? Iris knew he hadn't contacted Krista in several weeks, not since the divorce was made official. Adam never mentioned his dad, so she wasn't certain how they were getting on.

"Hey." She leaned back, smoothed Krista's dark hair away from her flushed face. "Would you be leaving me behind if you got a boyfriend?"

Confusion carved a sharp vee between Krista's brows. "No, but—"

"It's no different for me."

"I thought you said he wasn't your boyfriend."

"He's not. I'm making a point."

An almost pout formed on Krista's lips. She wasn't putting on too blatant a show, but obviously she wasn't ready to accept the argument Iris was giving her. That was fine. Iris could be content to let the seeds she'd planted sprout over time.

But any more time right now and she would be late to the library.

"Now," she said firmly, "I have to get ready for work. Why don't you head out, stop to get some coffee or something on your way to the office? You've got time."

Reluctance obvious on her face, Krista finally agreed to go, allowing Iris to breathe a sigh of relief. The interruption to her morning had her scrambling to get ready and reach the library before eight, but hopefully Krista would think about what had been said and this problem would finally start to dissipate.

Hopefully. But Iris had the feeling that hope was misplaced.

Thirteen

S ummer continued to pass in heated waves. Iris saw Jamie occasionally, when she happened to be meeting up with her friends for girls' night or when she stopped by Wildwood Brew for a coffee, though she didn't get the sense that he was stalking her. They talked, texted, but he didn't do more than give her a quick kiss or a casual lingering hand on her arm. Iris couldn't decide if she was relieved or disappointed.

Scarlett returned to Scotland with Gavin to work on her next book, leaving a hole that FaceTime just couldn't fill, but Iris knew her friend was happy, and that was all she could ask for, really. Though she missed her best friend, this dual life was a permanent situation, and Iris had vowed to get as used to it as she could, even if it left her feeling lonely at times. Lily and Claire and Erin welcomed her as an equal in their little group, but it wasn't the same as having Scarlett there. Still, Iris made the best of it.

She didn't speak of their morning argument with Krista again. The strained stalemate made visits awkward, but Iris was determined to give her daughter time to chew on the truths Iris had shared with her. And Iris was chewing on her own truths, like how much she enjoyed seeing Jamie each time they ran into each other. She didn't want to accept it, didn't want to be focused on one particular person, but even as she shared a random dance with another man at the pub on girls' night, she found herself constantly searching the crowd for a glimpse of his forest-green eyes.

One hot August evening, Iris timed herself out on the library's office computer with a sigh of relief. Thanks to a relatively quiet day, she'd been able to spend extra time in the back office, unpacking and cataloging the new arrivals. Her favorite part of the job. Glancing around, she felt satisfaction at the cleared space surrounding her. There would be more arrivals tomorrow, but for now she was all caught up.

Stretching her stiff muscles, she realized suddenly that she felt accomplished but not exhausted. For so many months now, the complications of her life, the changes had worn her down, dragged her into fatigue so that even the simplest task, the ones she enjoyed the most, were overshadowed by a depletion of energy she couldn't pull herself out of. Now, though, she felt almost like her old self. Like she'd found calm in her life. The emotional upheaval of the divorce no longer dominated her days and confused her nights. She felt…good, and she hadn't felt just plain good in a long, long time.

She liked it.

After retrieving her purse from the bottom desk drawer, she pushed in her chair and walked out to the check-out desk. Ashley sat at the front computer, casually flipping through a magazine as she waited for patrons to approach. "All set for the night?" Iris asked her.

The young woman gave Iris her usual bright smile. "All set!"

"Good." She settled her purse strap on her shoulder. "I'll see you tomorrow then."

"Have a good night," Ashley said.

Iris had almost made it to the front glass doors when one side opened and Jamie walked through. Dressed in a white button-down—with the sleeves rolled up those powerful forearms—and classic black slacks, he made her breath hitch in her throat. The rumpled state of his dress shirt and the tousled look of his hair, the red nearly overshadowed with salt-and-pepper, told her he'd been at the restaurant. He looked tired but, like her, satisfied with a hard day's work, and the way a smile lit up his face when he caught sight of her reflected her own jolt of pleasure as he entered the room.

"Jamie."

"Hey there, beautiful." Jamie beelined for her and brushed a casual kiss along her cheek, his usual greeting. She'd seen him greet Erin the same way, but she had a sneaking suspicion that the very attached and very pregnant Erin did not react the same way Iris did to that kiss. Everything inside her melted at the touch of his lips to her skin, and heat centered in her core in a way she was struggling more and more to ignore.

"What are you doing here tonight? Don't you have the dinner shift?" He typically did unless it was his night off, which seemed to be most often on Thursdays. She knew Michael took the night shift at the farm.

Jamie turned to face the doors, walking alongside her as she made her way out into the hot summer night. "Had to switch shifts with my assistant manager so he could have the day off for an appointment." His arm slid around her waist as naturally as breathing, his warmth enjoyable despite the sweat-inducing temperatures outside. "So I thought I'd drop by and see my favorite girl."

She smiled. "I thought Baby was your favorite girl."

There was that wicked grin. "She used to be."

He said things like that more and more. Iris tended to brush them off as casual flirting, but tonight she couldn't deny the ache in her chest that told her she wished it were true. She shouldn't—it was too dangerous to risk her heart with this man, or any man, for that matter—but she could no longer deny that the desire was there nonetheless.

Jamie paused on the sidewalk and drew her to a stop along with him. "Hey, what's that frown for?"

She stared into his eyes, intent on seeing…well, she wasn't sure, but she knew she was looking for something. "Why do you keep coming around to see me, Jamie?"

She was startled at the deep laugh that rumbled from his chest. "Only you would ask me that, Iris."

"Why?"

He brushed a finger across the tip of her nose. "Because you're you." He started walking again, pulling her along with him. "But for tonight, the reason I came around was to invite you to a day on the lake for the Fourth."

Her excitement at the invitation quickly fizzled at the timing. "I can't," she said, trying not to make her disappointment too obvious. "My son and his girlfriend are coming into town Friday for a week, and we already planned to spend July Fourth on the lake together."

"Bring them along!"

Jamie's enthusiasm made her smile, though that smile dimmed in the next moment. "Krista will be with us." Somehow the idea of introducing Adam to Jamie didn't bother her in the least, but her daughter spending time with him was another thing altogether.

They stopped at her car, and Jamie turned her to face him. "Iris…"

At his narrowed gaze, she swallowed hard. "What?"

His hand slid down her arm to tangle their fingers together. "Look, I know you're a smart woman, probably far smarter than me, so you have to know I'm not just coming around because I have nowhere else to be."

She would've protested, would've placed her fingers over those hard lips to halt the words she thought might be coming, but Jamie had effectively handcuffed her, holding one hand while the other carried her things from the office. And with the sudden lack of moisture in her mouth, talking was impossible.

"I want to spend time with *you*, Iris. I want to..." He seemed to swallow his words, then started again. "I want to get to know you, and not just because I want to be your friend."

Yes, she knew that, even if she'd tried to deny it. She hadn't been ready. She hadn't wanted to acknowledge what was happening because she'd been scared. If she was honest with herself, she still was, but not nearly as much as she should be to protect herself.

"Jamie, I—" How did you admit you were a coward? She swallowed against a dry throat.

"I know the timing isn't perfect," he said. "I know you may not be prepared to move forward yet. And I won't pressure you. But that doesn't mean I don't want to spend time with you."

She finally managed to squeeze out her greatest fear. "What if I'm never prepared?"

Jamie didn't balk, though, and he didn't seem disappointed, just shrugged. "Then you're not, and I've gained a better friend than I could ever hope to have." He used his free hand to brush the curls that covered her eye back, giving him an unobstructed view of her face. "But I'm betting that won't be the case."

He had far more confidence in her than she had in herself, at least where relationships were concerned.

Jamie broke the moment with that smile that always sent a zing through her. "Come on. We can cook out, swim at the dock, go out in my boat. It'll be fun."

"Even with Krista?" Her second biggest worry.

He winked. "She has to get used to me sometime."

Iris nibbled at her bottom lip.

"Just ask the kids about it and get back to me, okay?" He shook their joined hands playfully. "I'd love someone to spend the holiday with."

"Don't you have Michael?"

"Yes, but Michael's not as pretty as you."

That feeling she'd had before, in the office, the good feeling, came surging back, and she smiled. Despite every objection that came to mind, underneath it all, she really wanted to do this. "Okay, let me talk to the kids and I'll get back to you."

"Sounds nice." Jamie leaned in, and her breath caught in anticipation. He hadn't kissed her on the lips since the night Baby's foal was born, and despite her uncertainties, she'd missed it. Missed him. Missed the connection they'd seemed to have that night.

Jamie's lips met hers, and she opened instinctively. Jamie dipped his tongue inside. The sound that left him had her heart racing—a groan, as if he had missed this too. As if she tasted better than he remembered. And if the way he devoured her was any indication, both of those things were true.

After far too few minutes—and probably far too many, considering they were standing out in full public view—Jamie drew back. He was breathing heavy, and the sound brought a smile to her lips. He smiled too.

"Let me know," he said, the words hoarse, then turned toward his car. Iris watched him walk away, anticipation and flat-out lust sizzling in her veins. That kiss had thrown all her caution out the window. She hoped her kids were ready, because she couldn't wait to spend the day with Jamie on the lake, and she didn't think any objections would keep her from it.

She didn't stop smiling the entire drive home.

Fourteen

I ris didn't share how the conversation with her kids went when she talked to them about the lake visit, but if the mutinous look on Krista's face as she sat in Iris's front seat, pulling into the space next to his Mercedes, was any indication, it hadn't gone spectacularly. Jamie straightened his shoulders and forced the tension in his face to relax. He refused to let the young woman's disapproval get to him. Yes, he wanted Iris's family to like him, just as he wanted Michael to like Iris, but it wasn't a necessity. Nor would he start a war with Krista. He had every intention of being a part of Iris's life for a long time, and her daughter would simply have to get used to it. He had no doubt that he could eventually win her over, just like he was Iris.

The man exiting the car behind Iris's looked a lot like Kirk, but without the surliness Jamie remembered from the older man's face. Adam wore a smile that reminded Jamie much more of Iris than his father. He was Michael's age, Jamie knew, and lived in the Pacific Northwest. Iris's excitement at having her son home for a visit had been familiar. Although Michael lived on the property now, he had gone to college out of state, and Jamie remembered well the days of hoping for a visit from his son. He'd been thankful every day of his life for the close relationship the two of them shared.

Speaking of, Michael came to stand next to Jamie as their guests arrived. A low whistle left his son. "That one isn't happy to be here, is she?"

Leave it to Michael to say what Jamie was thinking. Jamie chuckled. "Krista has issues with her mother dating," he said, too quietly to carry to the cars.

Michael grinned. "Maybe I can distract her from her disapproval. Your woman was a real hottie in her younger days if her daughter is any indication."

"She's still a hottie," Jamie protested, using his son's word.

Michael laughed and clapped him on the back. "I didn't say she wasn't."

Jamie followed Michael to approach Iris's car. His son continued on to Adam's vehicle, introduced himself, and started the unloading process. Jamie listened with half an ear as he opened Iris's door. She was still sitting in her car, her attention on Krista, but whatever she'd been saying cut off as their privacy was ended.

Extending his hand to help her out of the car, Jamie gave Iris a reassuring look. "Welcome back."

"Hey, Jamie."

Wanting to set expectations up front but also refusing to embarrass Iris unnecessarily, Jamie directed his lips to her cheek instead of her mouth as he wanted. "I'm so glad you've come for the day."

Iris stepped back to encompass the rest of the crowd. "I was telling Krista about Baby. How is the foal doing?"

"Healthy as the horse she is," Michael said, joining them. "She's eating so much I swear she's trying to double in size every week."

"Not quite that much, but close," Jamie agreed. "Welcome to Flying Horse Ranch! I'd love for your family to meet Baby if they'd like." Maybe the horses would soften Krista up somewhat.

Adam and his girlfriend joined them, and Iris made introductions. "Jamie, Michael, these are my kids, Krista and Adam, and Adam's fiancée, Chloe."

"Fiancée?" Jamie reached for Adam's hand to shake. "Congratulations."

"Thank you," Adam said, his voice filled with pride. "She said yes just last night."

Chloe's light laugh filled the air between them. "Not that he had to be nervous about it or anything. He knew I'd say yes." She, too, shook Jamie's hand, then Michael's.

"I don't think a man is ever not nervous about asking a woman to marry him," Jamie said, adding, "A day on the lake is a great way to celebrate." He gestured toward the ATVs parked nearer the house. "Why don't we load up and we can stop at the barn on our way down to the dock. I'll come back up for the food when it gets closer to lunchtime."

A wave of enthusiastic replies came from everyone but Krista, who remained silent. Jamie, Michael, and Adam transferred supplies to the ATVs, Adam raving over the chance to drive one of them in the process. Jamie enjoyed the practicality of the vehicles on such a big farm, though he was too cautious to ride them recreationally. Fatal accidents with ATVs were far too common in the country. His one rule was that Michael wear a helmet if he went mudding with one—he refused to lose his son to a rollover accident. Adam had done a few tourist activities with similar vehicles, so Jamie felt confident in letting him drive himself and Chloe down to the dock. Michael took Krista, and Jamie practically purred as Iris snuggled up to his back, her lean, bare legs firm against his as she settled behind him. He let the others go a little ahead of them, waiting to turn the key until he'd had a private moment to turn and steal a kiss from the woman whose touch sizzled through his veins.

"Hi," he whispered roughly against her mouth.

Iris smiled, and he was pleased to note her voice was slightly breathless. "Hi, yourself."

"You look fabulous in shorts, by the way." Though her skirts definitely did her figure justice, he appreciated the extended view he was getting today. Very much, if the lack of room in his own shorts was anything to go by. He was beginning to wonder if Iris coming into his life was reversing the aging process, the way his body so frequently responded to hers. Not that he was complaining, though he did hope the evidence of his arousal would relax before they met the others at the barn. If Krista was upset with him now, sporting a stiff dick in front of her would make things ten times worse.

Iris dipped her head, her lips almost brushing his skin where his tank left his shoulder bare. He caught a glimpse of her smile before the fall of her bangs hid her face from view. "You too."

Surprise flashed through him. Iris never backed away from his affection, but there was something about her response today that had his heart speeding up. As if she'd turned a corner—or made a decision.

God, he hoped so.

He let one hand drop to her knee as he used the other to start the ATV and begin the short drive down to the barn. The others had walked through the long central area and out the back by the time they arrived, allowing Jamie a few more minutes with Iris alone. "Baby is out back in a secure pasture. Keeps the other horses away from the foal, but gives them room to run," he explained.

"What did you name her?"

He smirked. "In honor of the guest at her birth, her name is Daddy's Blossom."

Iris stopped, her hand going up to cover her open mouth. "You named her after me?"

Jamie slipped his arm around her waist and pulled her close. "Of course I did. You're the only flower I know."

"But Jamie…" She shook her head. "What if—"

He knew what she was thinking—what if they weren't together for long? What if she never got over her divorce? To him, none of that mattered. Leaning close, he put his mouth to her ear. "Don't you know I'd never want to forget you, Iris?"

And despite any reservations she might have, Iris relaxed against him. A soft sigh left her lips. "You're too good for me."

He chuckled. "No, I'm definitely not. I have all the faults other guys have." He eased back from her. "But you're worth working for."

He tangled their fingers together and led Iris out the back of the barn, back into the sunshine. A few feet away, leaning against the fence that surrounded the pasture, stood the rest of the crew, most of whom were focused on Baby grazing in the sunlight, Blossom at her side. All except Krista, who was staring their way. Jamie couldn't read her face behind the glare of the sun and her hat and sunglasses, but he figured if looks could kill, he'd probably be laid out on the ground by now.

Which was exactly why they ended up next to her at the fence.

Baby's sleek black coat gleamed in the morning light. Blossom was a reflection of her mother in every way aside from the blaze of white down the center of her forehead and the white socks on one front leg and one back. At Jamie's appearance, Baby knickered softly and began a slow walk over to the fence, Blossom following. Despite the crowd of people, she ambled straight to him and tucked her head over the fence to rest against his chest.

"Morning, Baby." He rubbed her cheek for a long moment, listening to the others chat about how beautiful Blossom was.

Michael filled in the details of how they raised their foals until Baby snorted and lifted her head. Jamie took a step back. "Say hi to Krista," he told the horse.

Krista caught her breath as Baby swung her big head in that direction. "Hold your hand out flat," Jamie murmured to her. "Let her catch your scent."

"Like a dog?"

Jamie ignored the irritation in her voice and instead nodded. "Just like that. Speak to her softly. You can watch her ears—if they are put back, she might be aggravated, but see how they are pointed right at you? She's curious."

Baby sniffed Krista's hand, her nostrils blowing hot streams of air with each breath. She brought her mouth to the tips of Krista's fingers and lipped at them but didn't attempt to bite.

Krista forgot her irritation long enough to giggle.

"It's okay to pet her neck."

As Krista became comfortable with the horse, Jamie stepped back, letting her have this moment. If anyone could win the young woman over, it was his Baby.

Smooth fingers surrounded his, and he looked over to share a smile with Iris.

Blossom, seeming not to want to be left out, had already gone over to Michael for attention. "She's so soft," Chloe said, petting the foal's neck.

Michael snorted. "Just be glad it hasn't rained in a couple of days. She discovered mud last week, and I had to give her a bath. She was coated in it."

"Kids do love mud puddles," Iris said. "I think Adam found every one within a mile radius around our house each time it rained. He was the king of mud pies."

"Good thing I didn't grow up to be a chef," Adam said.

"I can testify that mud pies are not a huge seller," Jamie put in.

They all shared a laugh, even Krista.

Blossom went back to nursing, and they decided to head down to the water. The dock had been present when Jamie bought the farm, but he'd added a boat house a few years ago to house the small boat they used for occasional fishing or skiing on the lake. Michael readied the boat and took the younger visitors out for a ride. Iris made herself comfortable on a lounge chair, and Jamie, intent on cooling himself off after the sight of Iris in her black swimsuit, dived into the water for a quick swim. They alternated activities until Jamie decided it was time to heat up the grill for lunch.

Michael took the ladies up to the house to grab sides and fixings while Jamie worked on hamburgers and steaks at the grill. The smell of charred meat and smoke had his stomach rumbling, but it was amusement that took over when Adam approached him, rubbing a towel across his dark hair. Though the look on the young man's face was friendly, Jamie could sense determination beneath the surface.

"How do you like your steak, Adam?"

Adam settled into a wide-legged stance on the other side of the grill, his big hands gripping his towel to hold it in a loop around the back of his neck. "Medium, usually, though Dad always burned them, so whatever you can manage that's edible is good for me."

Jamie let a bit of his amusement show. "I couldn't keep the Carousel open without knowing how to cook a steak to order."

Adam cocked a hip to one side. "Mom usually took over the grilling duties."

Jamie nodded. He had a feeling she'd taken over a lot of things to keep the house running smoothly during her marriage.

"So..." Adam cleared his throat. "You and my mom...um..."

He should probably put the man out of his misery, but it was too funny not to. "Me and your mom...?"

Adam scowled. "Talking about my mom and dating is...weird."

Jamie took pity on him. "Would it help if I told you I have no intention of hurting your mom, we are definitely taking things slow, and no, I won't discuss with you whether or not we intend to have sex? Although if we do, I will definitely use protection. Any other questions?" The bigger Adam's eyes got, the funnier Jamie found the whole thing. "You can skip the warnings, Adam, I promise. I want nothing more than for Iris to be happy."

"She didn't deserve what my dad did to her. And yes, I know the whole story," Adam clarified. "I knew something was wrong and finally just asked her outright; she answered honestly. Dad is a dick. I haven't spoken to him in months now."

Did Kirk even comprehend how much he'd lost with his selfishness? Jamie didn't think so. But Kirk's loss was definitely Jamie's gain.

"Kirk is a dick, I totally agree." He flipped a couple of patties on the grill. "Iris is a good woman, and I intend to treat her a lot better than your dad did, I assure you. As good as she deserves."

Adam's shoulders dropped, and he smiled, the gesture somewhat sheepish. "You better."

Jamie gripped one of the steaks with his tongs and prepared to transfer it off the grill. "I promise. And I keep my promises." He held up the steak. "Medium, right?"

Adam chuckled. "Medium. Perfect."

Fifteen

After a huge lunch that had them all groaning at the fullness of their stomachs, Jamie took the group out in the boat for a leisurely tour of the lake. Iris joined him in the seat next to his up front, the younger crew lining each side of the boat as they surveyed the coves around Douglas Lake and met up with other holiday goers celebrating the day off like they were. When they made it back to the dock, Jamie and Iris decided the lounge chairs sounded better than skiing, and left the "youngsters" to more energetic pursuits while they settled into the shade for naps.

Iris woke a short while later to the soft sound of snuffling snores from the chair next to her. The intimacy of hearing Jamie snore caused a melting in her heart. Knowing that small, secret detail about him emphasized the closeness they'd developed, just how far Jamie had managed to ease himself into her life and into her heart. And strangely enough, she wasn't panicking at the thought of a man being that close to her anymore. She was actually starting to be okay with it.

Did she want to marry Jamie? No, her aversion to getting married again was still strong. But she was intelligent enough to acknowledge that they already had some sort of relationship going on, and denying it wasn't going to make it untrue. Jamie was a part of her life. The question was, how much more of herself did she want to share with him?

Slipping from her chair, she glanced Jamie's way. The vulnerability of sleep made him look younger. It was as if the determination and drive he carried every second was let go for a little while, and his face relaxed, the tension around his eyes—whether from laughter or concentration—easing, allowing her to see a softer side of him than she'd seen before. Her fingers itched to touch him, to smooth back the wind-tossed hair along his forehead that stuck out at all angles, to run her fingers over that wide chest that she now knew was even more mouthwatering than she'd imagined it to be. Her gaze tracked down his long body, seeing all the bits of him that she never allowed herself to focus on for fear someone else might notice her interest.

Jamie Worthington was a handsome man indeed. And the warmth in her belly dared her to explore the deep masculinity on display before her in all the ways she'd dreamed about for months now.

Wanting to cool herself off—and yes, think about this decision that was presenting itself with a far cooler head than she was currently able to conjure—she lowered herself down the ladder on the other side of the dock and slipped into the chilly water of the lake. Here near the shoreline, the water was a clear green, allowing her to see through to the sandy bottom until it dropped off near the end of the dock to a much deeper depth. She lay out on her back, allowing the water to hold her, the sun hot above her head, the lapping water calm and cool around her. It felt good, shutting out the world and narrowing her focus down to only her body and her thoughts.

And one thought was rising above all the rest: she wanted Jamie Worthington, and she didn't want to wait anymore.

The longer she floated, the clearer the decision became. Did she have misgivings? Yes. She had never been with a man other than Kirk, and no matter how confident she was in herself, the idea of showing another man her body still gave her pause—or maybe even more so, given her age. But she was done letting her ex-husband and her past dictate her future and her feelings. Wherever this connection with Jamie took her, she was ready for the next step.

She was ready for sex. She hoped.

When she pulled herself out of the water, Jamie was still sleeping in his lounge chair, still softly snoring. She surrounded herself with a towel and walked over to stand at the end of his chair. Gently shaking her hair over his body showered cool droplets onto his skin, and Jamie stirred beneath her.

Sleepy green eyes focused on her, grazing her body with an intensity that almost had her squirming. "Hey," he said, voice rough with sleep.

"Hey, yourself," Iris said. "Did you know you snore?"

He laughed unselfconsciously, the sound doing funny things to her heart. "Sorry."

"Don't be." Iris scooted his legs to one side and settled onto the foot of his lounger. "It's nice to know you have a flaw or two."

"Oh, I have a flaw or two," he agreed, amusement clear on his face. "But from what Michael tells me, my snoring isn't loud enough you'd be forced to sleep in another room, away from me."

The idea that they'd sleep together enough for her to notice his snoring that way brought a delicate pink blush to her cheeks. Jamie's gaze fixated on her reaction and followed the flush of color with seeming fascination down the length of her neck, across her chest to the vee between the mounds of her breasts. Her breasts felt like they swelled under his attention, and her nipples peaked. She wondered if he noticed.

When she dropped her gaze to hide her thoughts, her glimpse of Jamie's lap told her he had indeed noticed—and responded.

He shifted a bit, drawing the towel next to him over his lap. Clearing his throat, he pulled her attention back to his face. "Are the kids back yet?"

"No," she answered absentmindedly, mulling over the past few seconds. Using the edge of her towel, she began to scrunch the water out of her curls. "They seem to be having fun."

"Good. I'm glad." Shifting up, he scooted toward her, his legs veed to admit her closer. Heat warmed her skin everywhere Jamie touched. "Are *you* having fun?"

"Yes," she said absently, not looking up at him. She switched to the other side of her hair, squeezing out the water, and the moment of quiet stretched out. Her gaze focused absently on her empty hand, which had automatically settled on Jamie's thigh. Her fingers traced lines along his skin, explored the rough texture of the hair on his leg. The deliciousness of the touch had her breath speeding up.

Jamie enjoyed it too—a shiver rocked him, and goose bumps rose along his skin. Did she really have that much power over this beautiful man, that a simple touch from her could make him shiver?

Jamie gripped a wet curl between a couple of fingers and gave it a playful tug. "What is it, Iris?"

She jerked her gaze up to his face. Green eyes captured hers, breathtakingly intense.

What was it? She opened her mouth, but no words came out. *I want you, Jamie. That's what it is. I want you so much.*

And in that moment, she stopped thinking and simply *did*.

Leaning close, she brushed her lips across his.

Jamie sucked in a breath. Could he could sense that this wasn't just a kiss, not simply taking advantage of the moment?

"Iris?"

She licked her lips. Moved in for another kiss. Only this one lasted longer—she opened her mouth and swiped her tongue across Jamie's full bottom lip.

That was all it took. Jamie opened as well, and then he was devouring her, his mouth hungry, his chest rumbling with the growl that rose up in his throat. The sound thrilled her—Jamie's pleasure, his need. Her nipples peaked, and she squirmed to get closer. Her fingers found their way into his hair, the short sides rasping along her skin. She trailed her hands down his neck, along his wide chest. He was so sexy he made her tingle, made her long to be touched as well—his fingers on her nipples, his chest against hers, his erection hard against her. It would feel so good.

The brush of her fingers across his tight nipples broke whatever restraint Jamie possessed, and he immediately took over. His hands came up to cup her face, his fingers driving into her hair to grip her head, tilt it until Iris was at just the right angle for him to dive deep. His tongue took over her mouth, his hunger a pulsing need between them that she could taste, feel, share. She wanted those hands on her body, on her breasts, between her legs. It was as if now that she'd finally acknowledged what she wanted, the desire had exploded tenfold into its true form, taking over every thought, every breath.

She wanted closer, wanted to feel his body fully against hers. Dropping her towel, Iris crawled up his body, not letting herself think, not allowing her misgivings to interrupt the onslaught of need. Instead she settled onto his lap, and those rough hands gripped her hips. Fingers hard, he dragged her forward until her core met the hard length of him for the very first time.

They fit just right. And oh God, it was just as good as she'd thought it would be. So good.

Her body knew what it wanted and sought it out without

conscious thought—her hips tilted to drag her clit against that solid length, giving them both the pleasure they sought.

They both groaned.

And that was when the sound of the engine registered in her brain.

Iris froze, unable to move. Jamie broke off their kiss with a curse. "You've got to be kidding me," he muttered under his breath.

A flush, this time of mortification, swept across her skin. "I'm sorry."

She forced her eyes open, afraid of what she'd see, but anger wasn't what awaited her. Frustrated amusement danced in those beautiful green eyes. "Well," Jamie said, voice low enough she could barely hear it over the boat's approach, "if you wanted to slowly introduce your kids to our relationship, I think that ship has sailed."

She held back a whimper of embarrassment. "I guess so." She began to move off Jamie's lap, but his hands were still gripping her hips, holding her in place. She frowned in question.

Jamie squeezed her hips, a question in both his grip and his eyes. "Maybe we could continue this later?" he asked softly.

The boat was pulling into the boathouse. She knew the kids were watching them, knew that Krista was judging, wondered what Michael thought of her sitting in his father's lap. Why she was allowing all of that judgment in instead of focusing on what she wanted, like she had moments before, she didn't know, couldn't suss out in the moment with all the chaos in her head. But she knew one thing—she wasn't ready for this to end.

"If that's okay with you," she whispered back. "I'd like that."

"Oh, there's no doubt I'd like that." Jamie gripped her head, pulled her in for a long, hard kiss, and then let her go.

As she scrambled off his lap, the kids came out of the boathouse and onto the deck. She didn't look at them, just gathered her towel and wrapped it around her rapidly cooling body, hoping no one would notice the state of her nipples. And then she looked to Jamie, saw him pulling his towel back across his lap.

Amusement broke through the chaos.

Jamie grinned as Iris started to laugh. "Think that's funny, do you?" he asked, cocking a brow in her direction.

"It's either laugh or cry," she whispered and stood up from the lounge chair. Gathering random plates and cups gave her something to do for the few moments she needed to gather her composure before facing their adult children, whose faces exhibited a mixture of amusement and horror.

But those few moments had given her something else: clarity. If the way she was feeling was any indication, their kids were going to have to get used to seeing Iris and Jamie together, just as she'd had to get used to it. Because they'd passed a turning point, and she didn't think there was any going back. She shrugged off the reactions and went to dump the trash into the trash can.

Sixteen

"You can ride back with your brother and Chloe," Iris assured Krista. "Their hotel is closer to your apartment than mine is, anyway."

"Mom—"

"Come on, Kris," Adam put in, throwing his arm around his sister's shoulders. "Let me give you a ride home."

"I rode here with Mom," Krista hissed at her brother.

"And you're riding home with me." Adam got that stubborn look on his face that he'd perfected through his teenage years. "Mom wants to hang out with Jamie a little longer, and there's nothing wrong with that."

"But—"

"Krista," Iris interrupted, grateful for Jamie's arm around her shoulders, lending his silent support. "I will see you in the morning. We've already got breakfast planned with Adam and Chloe before they leave."

Her son and his fiancée had a cabin rented for a little getaway of their own before they headed back to Seattle. As embarrassing as it was to argue with her daughter about staying to have sex with Jamie—not that she was explicitly saying that, but after their display on the dock, she had zero doubt everyone standing here knew what was going to happen between herself and Jamie tonight—at least the breakfast in the morning gave her a reason to see her daughter within an established timeline. She hoped that would suffice.

Not likely, but Iris wasn't giving in on this. She was an adult, and she'd made her decision.

Just the thought had her heart thumping with anticipation.

Adam was ushering his protesting sister over to his car, where he practically shoved her into the back seat. Chloe shot Iris a sympathetic look before giving her a little wave and getting into the car as well. "We'll see you in the morning, Mom," Adam called as he opened the driver's side door. Iris hoped her appreciation of his interference showed in the smile she gave him. Her son shot Jamie a salute and joined the others in the car.

She didn't move while the vehicle backed out, and gave the kids a wave as they headed down the driveway.

Finally. Her shoulders slumped in relief.

"Well," Michael said, voice cheeky, "I'll see you guys later." He turned to walk off, whistling.

"Not likely!" Jamie called after his son. "And don't come over for leftovers!"

"Jamie!"

Jamie laughed at her protest. "We have a very open relationship, trust me. And he *would* show up for leftovers if I didn't warn him." He gave her a squeeze. "I don't want that." He turned her in his arms to face him, ducking down until their eyes met. "I don't want anything to interrupt me from being with you—if that's what you're ready for. Did I read that right?"

"Yes," she said quietly, a blush hitting her cheeks. "Yes, you read that right."

Jamie let out a whoop. Without warning he lifted her off her feet to whirl her around. "What are we waiting for?"

Michael's laughter floated through the air from the door of the bunkhouse before he went inside and shut them out. Iris let a chuckle escape. "I think we were waiting for privacy, but since we have that…"

Jamie took her lips, his kiss long and sweet. When he finally released her mouth, his voice was rough with need. "I've been waiting a long time for this."

She cupped his cheek, her thumb gliding along his cheekbone. How had she managed to be gifted a chance with a man like him? "So I gather. I appreciate the patience."

He settled her back onto her feet and ushered her toward the door. "It's nothing less than you deserve."

The words softened her heart, and told her everything she needed to know about trusting Jamie in this moment. Her own husband had stopped caring about what she deserved, and yet here was a man who cared enough that he had kept his own desires on hold until she was ready. The thought shouldn't amaze her—it was basic human decency, right? She would do the same for him—but it did.

The secure clasp of Jamie's hand grounded her as they walked down the hall toward his bedroom. She'd been here before, but tonight was different. Tonight she would take her clothes off, give herself to Jamie in this room. She was grateful he didn't turn on the overhead light or the lamps near the bed —that might have made her feel like she had a spotlight on her. Showing Kirk her body had been easy; after all, he'd lived through all the changes time had wrought on her physical appearance along with her. Jamie hadn't. He was seeing all of her for the first time, and though she wasn't ashamed of her body, she also wasn't experienced enough to have zero concerns.

She shouldn't have. Jamie left her at the door, walked to the bathroom, turned on the lights, and closed the door halfway, giving them light to see but not so much that Iris felt self-conscious. There was enough light that the hungry look in his eyes was clear as he returned to where she stood, just inside the bedroom, and took her hand once more. Jamie walked her toward the bed. "Take off your shoes, Iris."

She slipped her sandals off. Jamie did the same, dropping his shoes and socks onto the floor beside the bed, then scooted up to the pillows. "Come here, beautiful."

The endearment made her smile. She crawled up the bed on hands and knees, watching Jamie watch her. Desire rose, and she gave herself over to it. When she reached Jamie, she leaned in and kissed him.

Jamie hummed with pleasure. Cupping her face, he held her to him, kissing her again, then again, as he guided her body down beside his. Lying together on the bed like this, fully clothed, reminded her of the times she and Kirk had made out as young adults, everything over the clothing until they'd been engaged, and even then they'd been careful not to go too far. She didn't have to restrain herself with Jamie—she knew where this was leading, and she couldn't wait.

Still, Jamie kept things PG long enough to drive her to frustration. She knew what he was doing, leading her into a mindlessness that would eliminate any misgivings, allow her to fully enjoy them being together without fear or worry. Still, it wasn't long before she was straining against him, arching her body into his touch, desperate for him to stop going slowly and take her clothes off, give her the touch she truly needed—against her bare skin, not with the barrier of their clothes separating them.

When a whine escaped her, Jamie chuckled. "Did you need something, baby?"

The smack of her hand against his chest was less playful and more irritated, which drew a full-on laugh from her partner. She opened her eyes and scowled at him. "Keep laughing and this isn't going to last long," she muttered, only half playful.

Jamie's grin didn't diminish, but he did cup her face and draw her in for a soft kiss. "I don't think it's going to last long anyway."

True, not if her body had its way.

"Undress me," she whispered against his mouth. It was something she could do herself, but she'd had dreams of Jamie taking off her clothes, revealing her skin inch by slow inch as he explored and admired.

Maybe Jamie had had those same fantasies, because his smile turned almost feral. "Gladly."

Her T-shirt was easiest. He raised it up her body slowly, gaze intent, taking in every inch that was revealed. She lifted her arms, and Jamie pulled the material over her head. When she could see again, he had eased down her body, his breath ghosting across her skin as he skimmed his mouth over her stomach. His tongue lightly traced stretch marks, pale silver now with age, the scar from her appendectomy—marks of the wars her body had fought. He came to the valley just below her breasts, and she sucked in a breath as he nipped at the front clasp of the bra she'd changed into after her shower earlier.

"Jamie."

Was that her voice, husky, needy? How long had it been since she'd felt drowned in desire?

So long.

"Iris." Deft fingers quickly opened the clasp, and Jamie wasted no time peeling back one cup, revealing a quivering breast topped with a rock-hard nipple.

"Please," she begged.

His wet tongue swept across the tip. Her back arched on instinct, doing its own begging.

When his lips closed over that aching point and sucked it inside his mouth, the relief was instantaneous. So was the hunger. She couldn't help it—she clasped his head, pulling him closer, begging for more with both her body and her words.

And Jamie obliged.

She wasn't certain when his fingers slipped under the soft skirt she wore and found the edge of her panties. She didn't care. All she knew was the need rising inside her. Jamie tugged gently, her underwear and her nipple, until she was writhing beneath him and her core was bare. And then a thick, hard finger found her center and slipped inside.

"Jamie!" Her legs fell open, her body arching convulsively.

His mouth left her breast. "That's my girl. Give yourself over, Iris." He thrust into her. The pad of his thumb found her clit, and Iris must have been much more primed than she realized, because all it took was another glide of his finger inside her, the hard press of his thumb, and she detonated just like that.

"Oh my God!"

He fingered her through her orgasm, driving her higher, wringing every last drop of pleasure from her body that it would allow. When she finally collapsed, he brushed his mouth over her panting lips. "Good girl."

She groaned, her body already stirring again just at his words. The bed moved as Jamie did something—removed his clothes, maybe? She was too blissed out to look, but the next thing she felt was rough hair, smooth skin, and hard muscles against her body. Jamie tugged her skirt down until she was naked, then aligned them together. The quiver that rocked him filled her with a feminine confidence she'd never known before.

He tucked his face into her neck and groaned. "Iris."

She ran her hands down the length of his bare back. "Do you have condoms?"

"I damn well do," he rasped. Rolling backward, he

reached for the bedside table. When he rolled back, he held a silver packet between his fingers.

Wanting to give him pleasure the way he had her, she took the condom from him. "Let me." Pushing against his shoulder, she eased him onto his back and, ignoring the self-consciousness that tried to rise, moved over him until she was straddling his legs. The thick, hard penis rising so close to her core made her mouth water.

She had the condom covering him in less than a minute, and though she wasn't strictly ready for another orgasm yet, she wanted him inside her, wanted to feel him filling her up, and so she eased above him and slowly drove her body down onto his. Her core opened around him, a snug fit that felt oh so good. When she looked to his face, Jamie's eyes were squeezed shut, his breath panting, and as that last few centimeters entered her body, he arched beneath her, his expression telling her he couldn't resist even if he'd tried.

The head of his cock hit the back of her, and they both groaned. "Oh God, Jamie."

His fingers bit into her hips. "Give me a minute."

She chuckled, though the sound was strained. Her legs settled on either side of his hips, and she felt her clit mash into the hair at his pelvis as she let her weight rest on him. A moan rose in her throat.

A curse left Jamie's mouth.

Iris waited there in the quiet, closing her eyes. Her focus went to her core, to the pulse of Jamie's body inside hers, the feel of him breathing beneath her. After half a minute or so, a sigh left him, and his hands rose to stroke her sides, her stomach, her breasts. She opened her eyes.

Jamie was watching her, gaze intent, eyes narrowed. His fingers pinched lightly at her nipples, stopping her breath. "Okay?" he asked.

"I should be asking you that." Planting her hands on

either side of his shoulders, she leaned over and brought their mouths together. "You feel perfect inside me."

The kick of his erection told her how much he appreciated her words. "You feel perfect around me, Iris." One hand continued its attention at her breast, and the other dropped to push between their bodies until he found her clit. "I can't wait, beautiful."

She lifted just enough to allow him access. "Me either." As she kissed him, she rolled her hips, rising along his length, then dropping down. Jamie kissed her back, the movement desperate, and thrust up hard into her next drop. Again and again their bodies met, their tongues tangling, as Iris chased the high she knew Jamie could give her. It wasn't long before he pulled his mouth away. "I can't—"

"Come, Jamie. It's all right. Come for me." She quickened her pace, rising and falling, and felt the beginning of her own climax just on the horizon. Jamie gripped her hips, pulling and pushing, and his orgasm struck, arching his body, straining every muscle as it took him over. Iris fought his hold, continuing her ride, continuing to strain until she, too, went over the edge, falling into the abyss of pleasure alongside the man beneath her.

The man she hadn't been looking for. The one she didn't want to let go. Not now. Maybe not ever.

Seventeen

Jamie woke, spooned tightly behind Iris's back, after a long night of sleep—and other things—just like he'd dreamed of for months. He'd known that when Iris finally let him in, she would be the sweetest he'd ever tasted, and last night had proved him right. Not that he'd had a chance to taste her, but it was definitely on his wish list.

Lord, she felt so good in his arms. He never wanted to let her go. But he couldn't say that, not yet. She might have given him her body, but pushing for more would only scare her off. Better to let her get used to the vulnerability between them first.

Dawn was just peaking over the horizon, lightening the cream curtains and giving the room a faint glow that echoed off of Iris's bare shoulder. He brushed a kiss over that creamy skin, breathed in her scent—woman and sex and something sweet—and forced himself to slide out of the bed, pad across the room, and enter the bath to get cleaned up.

When he exited, tugging his T-shirt over his head, Iris was just stirring in the bed. He smiled as she rolled onto her back and shot a frown his way. "It's too early to get up."

He moved to her side of the bed, his heart skipping a beat

at the thought—*her side of the bed.* "You can drift back off if you want."

"What time is it?"

"Almost seven."

She shook her head. "I need to swing by the apartment before I meet the kids this morning, change clothes."

"Want some coffee?"

"God, yes." The frown reappeared. "I'm not a morning person."

He chuckled. "You don't say." He pressed a short, sharp kiss to her lips before she could protest, then moved back. "Bathroom is all yours if you want to shower. Work out some of the kinks?"

She pushed up to sit, and a groan left her lips. "How did you know?"

"That you'd be sore?" He admired the view of her bare breasts in the morning light. "Good guess."

"Mmm." Iris raised her arms high, seeming unselfconscious about the view she provided as she stretched. Or maybe she was teasing him. The satisfied smile she shot his way could mean anything. "Hot water does sound good. You'll make the coffee?"

He adjusted himself behind the fly of his jeans. "Unless you want company."

"Not before I brush my teeth."

Her response made him laugh. "How did I know you'd be a 'let me brush my teeth first' woman?"

"Because you're smart." She stood, and he got his first glimpse of the full length of her naked body in the daylight. If he'd thought his zipper was tight before, that was nothing compared to now. "Give me five minutes."

He watched her cross the room, displaying a mouthwatering backside that made his breath come quicker, but he didn't move. Instead he watched the clock on his side of the bed, ticking down the minutes. Just as the second hand moved into place, the door to the bathroom opened. Iris didn't say anything, didn't peek through, but the door left ajar was an invitation he wasn't about to turn down.

How had he gotten lucky enough to find this woman and claim her for himself?

Iris waited inside the walk-in shower, the warm water falling on her upturned face. Arms raised, fingers pushing the thick fall of her bangs back, she was a goddess waiting for her lover. Waiting for him. A shiver shook him as he undressed, his dick aching with a need that had nothing to do with the divine. Iris awakened a hunger in him that he hadn't felt in a long time. She made him want, not just the physical act of penetration, but the feel of silken skin and a warm mouth, a tongue dancing with his, heavy breasts resting in his hands, against his lips. He wanted all of her, and he wanted it now. Last night hadn't been nearly enough to sate him.

Sliding into the shower behind her, he breathed in the steam and heat. He moved in close, nestled his rigid shaft along the small of her back. The wet glide of her skin against him kicked his desire up another notch. Arms closing around her waist, he pulled her tight against him and dropped his mouth to the slope where neck met shoulder. "Iris," he groaned against her skin. Droplets of water awaited his tongue, and he lapped them up one by one, feeling Iris shift against him, her back arching to give him access. The flesh of her stomach had that distinct feminine curve from belly button to mound, the one that testified to the babies she'd carried inside her—he traced a line down, down, down until he reached her center, then flattened his palm and began a slow massage designed to heighten her need to the same level as his.

"Oh." Iris widened her stance, allowing him deeper. It wasn't enough for him. He hooked the back of her knee and lifted, settling her foot on the low bench that made up one wall of the shower, and gloried in the access it gave him. All those delicate folds and crevices awaiting the simple glide of his fingertips that could bring Iris so much pleasure.

This wasn't like last night. Oh, he'd taken his time seducing her, but once they'd gotten their clothes off, there had been no stopping the rush to the finish. This was lazy, leisurely, easygoing and oh so good. He could feel the slick glide of cream between Iris's legs, the evidence of her arousal, hear the gradual increase of her breath as excitement rose. The rocking of her pelvis against his fingers became more and more deliberate. Iris sought out the touches that brought her the most pleasure, teaching him how to arouse her, what worked for her and what didn't. He studied each and every move, a willing student of her guidance even as his own tension rose higher and higher. But he held on, focusing on her, until her soft cries turned to begging.

"Jamie, please. Please!"

Shifting back a couple of steps, Jamie took Iris with him, giving them space, then pressed a firm hand against her back to bend her over. Instinct had her placing her hands on the shower wall, her spine a gorgeous arch before him and that amazing ass on full display. He lined himself up, then hesitated. A curse left him.

"What is it?"

"I forgot a condom," he explained, voice rough with need.

"Oh." Rising, Iris turned to face him. "Um…"

He pulled her close. "I can run get one."

She hesitated, uncertainty in her eyes. "Have you—" She cleared her throat. "Have you been tested…um…recently?"

She hadn't had this conversation before, he could tell. Of course she hadn't. But he was proud of her for standing up for her safety instead of giving in to what she might think he wanted. "I have." He traced a thumb along the full line of her lips. "After the first time I kissed you. I wasn't taking any chances."

The tension in her shoulders relaxed. "Really?"

"Really." His lips quirked into a grin. "I have the printout to prove it, too."

She smiled. "Me too."

Surprise shot through him. "Really?"

"Really."

"What about birth control?" he asked.

"I had to have a hysterectomy when I was forty."

No chance of getting pregnant then. "So…"

She tipped her head. "So…"

He squeezed her waist. "You're going to have to say it, Iris."

Her teeth caught her lower lip, and he thought for a moment she wouldn't tell him what she wanted, but his woman was braver than that. "You can take me without a condom, Jamie."

This time it was his tension that released. He took her mouth hard, exploring, tangling, tasting until they were both breathless. Only then did he release her. "Are you absolutely certain?" Because he'd get himself out in the damn cold air to get a condom if it meant the difference between having her and not.

Her stare was candid, rock steady. "I'm absolutely certain."

"Thank God."

"Hey," she said, turning herself around and throwing him a look over her shoulder, "shouldn't it be me you're thanking?"

"Oh, I'll thank you, all right." And he did—with his fingers, his tongue, in every way he could imagine, until she was back to begging and he had her bent over before him. The heat of her core enveloped his dick, so intense he had to pause before he lost all control. And then he was sliding inside, feeling every subtle nuance of her body, every shift and breath. The head of his cock met that sweet spot just under her cervix, and her breath choked off.

"That's it, beautiful." He retreated, advanced, making certain to rub that spot with each entry. "That's it." He gripped her hip hard with one hand. With his other, he reached beneath her and palmed a breast, thumbing her hard nipple to heighten her pleasure. Iris arched into his touch with a cry. "That's good. So good, Iris." He crooned to her, feeling her body tighten down on his shaft, feeling her cream coat him as her pleasure rose. "Come on, beautiful. Come for me."

Iris pushed back against him, straining, straining. Jamie fought to hold on, to hold off. He brought his hand to her clit, and with one press of his finger circling her most sensitive spot, she let go.

"That's it." The words were strained, a hoarse declaration of both her own pleasure and his. That delicious peak overtook him. Iris pressed against the wall, forcing herself as close as she could get to him, even as he pressed forward, body shaking with each jet inside her. The knowledge that he was bare mixed with his climax, threatening to blow off the top of his head. By the time he finished, he was slumped over her, holding them both up by some barely remembered instinct, knowing only that he didn't want to slip from her body until he absolutely had to.

Long minutes later, they slumped to the bench together.

"Jamie." Iris's voice was husky, and damned if that didn't make him a little proud. "This is…"

He waited for her to find her words.

"This is so much more than I expected."

When she didn't elaborate, he spoke over the thumping of his heartbeat. "Is that good or bad?"

A faint smile touched her lips. "Good." She raised sated eyes to him. "I can't say it doesn't scare me, but I'm not going to run."

He leaned in, unable to resist the need to take her mouth, take her promise direct from her lips. "Thank you."

Her smile became a full-on grin. "You got it right this time."

"Hey, I know who to thank." He matched her grin. "Especially if you tell me we can do this again."

"Yes, we definitely can."

He slid from the bench onto his knees and positioned himself between her legs. "Then I'll have to perform a proper thank-you."

Her eyes went wide. Iris straightened on the bench. "Will you?"

"I definitely will." He'd wanted to taste her, and he wasn't about to let the opportunity pass. He licked the side of one knee. Her thigh. Higher. "Hold on tight."

A long time later, Iris's "you're welcome" was barely audible, but it was the smile on her face that told him everything he wanted to know.

Eighteen

As she rushed through the rain into Wildwood Brew, Iris was especially thankful for Jamie's firm massage this morning after their shower. She felt like her body was singing. Every muscle and joint that had been sore this morning now moved with a fluidity that only pleasure and Jamie's touch could have given her. And she had a definite smile on her face. Jamie had made sure of that —last night and this morning.

A sigh of contentment left her as she made her way toward the counter, shaking off raindrops along the way. When had she last felt content? Before the divorce? A very, very long time. Things had gone from fine to strained to estranged over years, not days. She'd spent a lot of those years walking on eggshells without even realizing it. Looking back over the summer, though, she realized she'd felt contentment creeping in repeatedly. She liked her life. She liked Jamie. It wasn't how she'd imagined the second half of her life would be, but she'd healed enough that she was no longer afraid to say this life was *good*.

She claimed a seat on the couch near the front window and tilted her head back against the cushions, closing her eyes to listen to the falling rain hitting the glass, savoring the moment and the feelings so newly awakened inside her. The sound of a throat clearing broke through her revery a few minutes later.

She opened her eyes to Maria, the owner of Wildwood Brew, standing before her, coffee in hand. "Sorry. I was lost in thought, I guess."

"Don't be." Maria extended her drink with a wink, brown eyes twinkling. "Looked like they were good thoughts."

Iris blushed. Maria chuckled her way back to the front counter.

A few blows of her breath cooled the coffee enough for a sip. She was savoring the first taste when Adam appeared outside, hurrying up the sidewalk. He was alone. Dread began to creep around the edges of her morning's bliss.

He stopped just inside the door to shake off the raindrops like she had when she'd arrived, before crossing the room toward her. "Good morning, Mom."

"Good morning." She gratefully accepted his hug. "Where's Chloe this morning?"

Adam shrugged. "She wanted to give us some mother-son time."

She cocked her head, looking up at him. "Did Krista also want to give us some mother-son time?" He'd been tasked with picking his sister up, she knew.

Adam's grin was wry. "No. She just wanted to make you sweat."

Her palms could attest that the tactic was working. "And you?"

She thought she knew the answer, but she held her breath as Adam drew her in for a half hug, pulling her to his side. He winked. "I'm just here for the coffee."

She laughed, relief relaxing her shoulders. At least she could have a pleasant few moments with her son before handling the problem of Krista. "Me too."

Adam went up to the counter to order and spent a few minutes talking to Maria and her daughter, DeeDee, in the quiet coffee shop. He'd visited Black Wolf's Bluff before, so both ladies knew him. When he returned, it was with a plate of fresh, warm, perfectly crunchy chocolate croissants with soft, gooey centers. Her favorite. "These just came out of the oven according to Maria," he said. "Claire brought them over from the bakery a couple minutes ago."

"Yum." Iris swore she could tell the difference between Claire's cooking and anyone else who worked at Gimme Sugar next door, which might become a problem if Claire decided to shift permanently to overseeing the new bakery up at the Black Wolf's Bluff Resort and hand the reins of the shop in town over to someone else. Iris would have to make trips up the mountain to get her fix—Claire's baking was definitely worth it.

She ate a bite of the pastry and swallowed it down with the dark roast coffee she preferred in the morning. Amusement had filled her when she joined Jamie in the kitchen this morning, only to see a bag of Wildwoods Brew special dark roast blend on his counter beside the coffeepot. He liked good coffee, too, apparently. This was her second cup, and though Jamie did a good job of making it, no one made it quite like Maria. Another sip had her humming and lying back on the couch to rest her head in the dim light filtering through the rain outside the window.

"I like that smile, Mom," Adam said quietly. Earnestly. Iris opened her eyes to look at her son. "I haven't seen a smile like that on your face in...well"—he rubbed a hand across his forehead—"in a long, long time."

Since the divorce. An ache started up in her chest. The damn divorce was always there in the background like a spider, waiting to catch a fly in its web. Which was to be expected, she guessed. That didn't mean she wasn't upset when they tripped over a moment like this.

But there were better things in her life now. After last night, *very* good things. Wanting Adam's take on her situation, she admitted, "Jamie is good for me, I think."

Adam nodded her way. "I'd say so if that hickey was anything to go by."

"What?" Her hand flew up to her neck, searching frantically for any tender spots. Adam managed to hold it together for a few moments before he started laughing.

"Sorry, Mom. There's nothing there. You don't have to worry."

She narrowed her eyes his way. "Michael already likes to poke fun. In a good way, I promise," she was quick to add at Adam's sudden scowl. "But we don't need two of you giving us a hard time."

Adam relaxed, laughed around the coffee cup at his lips. "Sure you do; the more the merrier."

"No, we don't." She swatted his knee. "Behave."

Her son laughed even harder. "Oh, you definitely have me confused with someone else."

Oh Lord, what had she unwittingly unleashed? She rubbed at the sudden ache between her eyes, but a reluctant chuckle left her, mingling with her son's hearty amusement. They shared a look that mingled mutual understanding and the knowledge of just how annoying Adam had been as a teen and young adult, allowing the laughter to fade into a companionable silence. The rain added contentment as they sipped their coffees together.

The moment felt good.

When he finished, Adam caught Maria's attention with a raised hand. One eyebrow lifted in Iris's direction. "More?"

Iris hesitated but finally shook her head no. She was buzzed enough.

When Maria signaled back a few minutes later by raising a new cup in the air, Adam walked up to the counter to retrieve the second offering. Iris watched him talking with Maria, and a swell of pride hit her. Her marriage to Kirk hadn't lasted "till death do us part" like she'd expected, but two admirable, self-sufficient adults had resulted from it. Or normally admirable. A sigh left her as Adam settled back into his seat.

"What's that frown about?"

Her face had always shown her emotions pretty clearly—and Adam had always read her better than his father. "Your sister."

Adam sighed too and sipped his coffee thoughtfully. The cream, once a perfect swan on the surface of the drink, formed a foaming mustache on his upper lip. "She'll come around eventually."

Iris's brows shot up. "Right. You didn't see her when she caught me coming home from Jamie's house the morning after Blossom's birth."

Adam snickered. "The walk of shame, huh?"

She gifted her son with a mock death glare. "If I'd slept with Jamie then—and I didn't, not that it's any of your business—there would have been nothing to be ashamed of."

Adam reached to squeeze her hand, a quick, conciliatory smile on his face. "Of course not. Just teasing, Mom."

"*Anyway*"—Iris shook her head, the memory playing out in her mind—"she had an absolute fit. It was…" She winced. "At this point, she's had the summer to get used to him being around. We've gone from full-out tantrums to the silent treatment."

"That's progress!"

Considering the alternative, he wasn't wrong. Still… "Not good progress."

Adam sat back, rolling his head against the couch. "I don't know, Mom." His gaze focused on the ceiling, and this time he was the one who frowned. "Dad fucked everything up, didn't he?"

That ache in her heart returned. So much had been destroyed because of one man's dissatisfaction. At times the sadness of that still hit, like now, seeing her son's grief. But her emotions no longer hit a stop sign there; she could walk herself past it, into a future that, though it didn't include her husband of so many years, could still hold happiness. Pleasure. Joy.

"He did," she finally agreed. Adam turned his gaze in her direction. "But it doesn't have to stay fucked up."

Adam's brow rose at her use of his word. The mother he'd known never cursed.

A lot had changed since then.

She reached over and smoothed a finger along his eyebrow, tracing the dark arch. "What he did changed all our lives, but I'm okay now," she assured him. "I'm happy." She thought of Chloe and the joy she'd given Adam. "You're happy."

Adam hesitated, took her hand, and gave the back of it a kiss. "Now we just have to get Krista happy."

Iris shook her head and sat back, sighing. "We can't get her there. It's something only she can do." That was the problem—Krista had to *want* to get past this, and Iris didn't know if she ever would. She drank down the last sip of her coffee. "That's what I'm afraid of."

Nineteen

I ris had agreed to dinner at Lily's house with her friends the following Tuesday night, for which she was grateful. Hopefully it would keep her mind off her daughter. And Jamie. Because now that they'd been together, he was even more dominant in her thoughts, but Jamie was working tonight and she couldn't let him take up all her brain space—or her life. She wouldn't let any man take over like that again.

No matter how good the sex—and everything else—was.

"Iris!"

Claire's squeal as she opened the door pierced Iris's eardrums. She stuck a finger in one ear and jiggled it around. "Eh? What's that you said?"

Claire laughed. "Sorry! A little too excited there, huh?" She opened the door wide, gesturing Iris in. "Lincoln comes into town tomorrow and construction at the resort has this week off, so I opted to close everything and do the same. I haven't taken time off in ages. I've been buzzing all day."

Iris gave her friend a hug. "I totally get that."

"Good, because I'll probably be just as loud when Erin gets here."

"Maybe I'll go see if Lily needs help in the kitchen."

Claire's laughter followed her down the hall, bringing a smile to Iris's lips. She didn't know what she would do without these women who had gathered around her since the divorce. So many of her friends had dropped off the radar as soon as they heard the news, as if divorce was contagious and they didn't want to catch it. Not Scarlett, though. They'd become close after working together at the Halloween event last year, and the other woman had pulled Iris into this circle as if she belonged here. By now she felt like she did.

Lily was putting together a charcuterie board when Iris entered the kitchen. "Ooooh, cheese straws!"

Lily grinned. "And Claire brought them, so you know they're good."

"What does she call them again? Cheese cookies?" Iris dared to reach for one of the small orange circles that were indeed shaped like cookies.

"Yeah." Lily added pretzels to the tray. "She says that's what her family always called them."

"They're delicious," Iris said around a mouthful of fluffy, cheesy goodness.

"Yes, cheese cookies!" Erin hurried through the kitchen door, one hand supporting her bulging stomach, the other reaching for a cookie.

Claire snorted as she followed Erin into the room. "Maybe I should have brought more."

"Yes!" Erin declared, mouth full of cheese cookie. "So we'd have leftovers to take home."

Lily finished laying out the food while Iris poured drinks; then they all sat at the kitchen table to eat. It took no more than two bites for Lily to say, "So, Iris, anything you want to tell us?"

"Yeah," Claire threw in, wiggling her brows. "Anything at all?"

Iris gave them both a frown. "Like what?"

Erin sat back in her chair, rubbing up and down along her belly as if it ached. "We want to know how Jamie was in bed."

Iris choked on her sip of sweet tea. The table erupted in laughter.

It took a few minutes to get herself back under control. When she lifted her brows at Erin, her friend shrugged. "Hey, we were all thinking it; I just said it out loud."

Iris eyed the other two women. "*Were* we all thinking it?"

Lily looked abashed. Claire did not. "Of course we were." She flashed white teeth at Iris.

"How in the world could you all know...?"

This time it was Lily who spoke. "You have that special glow about you."

"I do?" Self-consciously she touched her cheek.

"You do," Erin assured her, more serious this time, reaching across the table to clasp her wrist in a warm hold. "And it looks beautiful on you."

Iris felt a blush rise to her cheeks. "Thank you. And..." She giggled at the three pairs of expectant looks aimed her way. "Everything went fine."

"Fine?" Claire smacked Iris's arm playfully. "Is that all we get, 'fine.'"

"Yep." She picked up a pretzel and, before popping it into her mouth, admitted, "All three times."

Her friends erupted with hoots and hollers.

"I definitely miss the nights when three times were involved," Erin said, continuing to rub her belly. A grimace twisted her mouth. "Yesterday my doctor recommended I have sex to start labor, and I just looked at her like she was crazy. I mean, what the hell are you talking about?"

"Right?" Iris chuckled. "Sometimes I think even OBGYNs forget that at the end of pregnancy, the last thing you feel is sexy."

"More like a hippo," Erin complained.

Lily reached for her friend, rubbing her shoulder comfortingly. "You don't look like a hippo. You look like the happiest woman in the world with the cutest baby mound ever. I know I'm really excited for this next chapter in your life."

"Exactly," Claire said. "We get baby time!"

"Why do you guys get to enjoy baby time and I am the one who had to go to all the trouble to produce the baby?"

Laughter rippled around the table. "Hey," Lily said, "you're the only one of us who's going to go through this. We have to get our secondhand enjoyment somehow."

"And we get to hand the baby back when it starts to cry," Claire said. "Win-win!"

Erin grinned. "Y'all stop."

"What does Carter think about things?" Iris asked. "And Thad?"

"Thad cannot wait. I swear, he FaceTimes me every day now that he's home with his mom, begging to know when his little sister is gonna be here. He can't seem to grasp the concept that nagging is not going to get me to go into labor."

Iris shot her a sympathetic grin. "At least he's a child. My husband was the nag. By the time Adam finally arrived, I was exhausted just from all the many suggestions he had to get me to go into labor. I swear I walked three miles a day, every day, for the ten days past my due date—at Kirk's insistence."

Claire rolled her eyes. "You could've followed Erin's doctor's advice and just had sex every day."

"As much as I would normally jump on that idea—and my husband"—Erin shifted uncomfortably in her seat—"I would really rather walk three miles every day at this point."

Discussion turned to the new bakery and the work Claire was doing to get it up and running. Portions of the new resort would be opening in two months, and Claire wanted Gimme Sugar Too to be ready by then. Lily talked about issues with the city council, which Iris commiserated with. They were due for another council meeting next week, an event Iris dreaded every month. Kirk was still a member, so it meant not only seeing him every month, but sitting next to him since they had traditionally been assigned those seats together before the divorce. It was nerve-racking and stress inducing. Ever since the news of his engagement, she kept her fingers crossed that he would decide to leave the city council and focus on his new wife. She wasn't holding her breath, though; the past couple of months she got the feeling that he might stay just to get on her nerves. Because of course he would.

They finished eating and were taking their drinks into the living room to relax when Erin suddenly clutched her stomach, one hand reaching for the wall to steady herself. A low moan escaped her.

"You okay, Erin?" Claire asked, reaching for her friend.

"Just a hard one," Erin said, voice strained. "These Braxton Hicks have been a bitch lately."

"Are you sure that's all they are?" Iris asked.

"Pretty sure." Erin panted a minute longer, the strain on her face relaxing as the contraction eased off. With a deep breath, she straightened to full standing.

A gasp left her.

Claire was right back in there. "What is it?"

Erin looked down. "I think my water just broke."

As one, they all looked down to see a wet streak along Erin shorts and down her leg. "Oh, sweetie," Lily said. "I'll get a towel."

Claire looked to Iris, her eyes frantic. "What do we do?"

Iris grinned at the other woman. "We have a baby." She moved to take Claire's place at Erin's side. "Why don't you give Carter a call?"

Claire nodded, rolling her eyes. "Of course I should give Carter a call." She relinquished her hold on Erin and rushed for the living room.

Iris stepped up to her friend. Erin met her eyes, her own filling with tears.

"What's wrong?" Iris asked. "Don't cry. It's gonna be okay." She reached to rub a tear from Erin's cheek.

"I'm not ready," Erin said, the tears coming stronger, more quickly.

Iris gave her a hug. "You're more ready than you feel, trust me." She moved to stand in front of Erin, clasping her friend's shoulders. "I know it feels overwhelming right now, with the whole thing looming in front of you. But you're both gonna do great, and your baby is going to be here in no time at all. You both will be fine."

Erin soaked in the words like they were a lifeline. Then the next contraction hit. "Oh!"

Iris turned her toward the wall, guiding her hands up to lay flat against it. "Lean over a little bit, Erin. Let the wall take your weight."

She rubbed Erin's back through the contraction, murmuring soothing nonsense words that even she didn't understand, knowing Erin wouldn't really hear any of them, just the tone. Already her focus was moving inward, concentrating on her body, on her baby. The sight brought back so many memories for Iris, the moments she'd spent laboring to bring Adam and Krista into the world. The thought of her daughter squeezed at her heart. So much time had passed between their births and now, so much had changed, but that single-minded love that was born when your child was conceived never went away.

Iris coached Erin through the contraction, then handed her over to Lily to clean up a bit while they waited for Carter to arrive. Twenty minutes and four contractions passed before the squeal of brakes in the driveway reached them. Carter was at the door seconds later. "Erin?"

"Here!" The word was a harsh rasp as Erin panted through a contraction.

Carter rushed to her side, his lips meeting her temple, his arms wrapping around his wife and the belly that held their baby. "It's okay, just breathe." He whispered in her ear through the long moments of squeezing pain, and when they passed, a little smile appeared on his face. "Our baby's coming," he said more loudly, words full of wonder.

"She is," Erin said. She straightened up. "We need to go."

They bundled Erin into Carter's car and watched the two of them back out, headed for the hospital. Nostalgia tugged at Iris as she imagined their next steps, the moment when Baby Deveraux would take her first breaths in this world. So much love and laughter lay ahead of them.

Claire, Lily, and Iris went back inside, poured some wine, and toasted their friends' new beginning as they waited for news.

Twenty

Instinct had Jamie reaching for Iris's hand as they crossed the parking lot toward the front entrance of the hospital. He'd craved her touch from the minute he met her, but now that she'd given herself to him, whenever she was with him he couldn't stop. Holding her hand, putting his arm around her waist, a kiss anytime he could sneak it in. And it was never enough.

He squeezed her fingers lightly. "Erin said everything went fine with the delivery?"

"Picture perfect." A glance showed him that Iris was smiling softly. "Longer than she wanted, I'm sure, but that's true of every delivery. She gets to go home tomorrow as long as the baby continues to do well."

They entered the hospital through the heavy sliding glass doors and crossed the neutrally painted lobby that was supposed to make everyone feel calm. Jamie had always hated hospitals. He could still remember Michael's birth like it was yesterday, the chaos and the anxiety and the waiting. It didn't matter what color the walls were, there was nothing about the whole experience that had felt calm. But he was certainly glad Erin and Carter had managed all right.

The elevator took them to the labor and delivery floor, and they made their way through the maze of hallways to Erin's room. Iris knocked on the door and pushed through when Carter's voice called for them to enter.

"Congratulations!" Iris hurried across the room to give Erin a hug. Jamie followed, holding the flowers he'd picked out and the gift Iris had brought along. Carter stood to the side of Erin's bed, a bundle wrapped in a soft pink blanket held securely in his arms. He reached to shake Jamie's hand.

"How are you feeling?" Iris asked, the question directed at Erin.

"Sore," she admitted, a tired smile taking over her face. "But happy."

"Want to meet the baby?" Carter asked, his voice coated in proud-dad energy.

"Absolutely." Iris tucked back the blanket with gentle fingers, revealing the baby's sleeping face. A flush of dark fuzz coated her head, dark lashes lying long against rounded baby cheeks. Her pink rosebud mouth moved gently as if suckling in her sleep.

Jamie leaned forward, getting a good look but being careful not to hover too close. "Hey there, little one," he said, his voice gruff.

"What's her name?" Iris asked.

"Rayne." Carter shared a loving glance with his wife. "We wanted to connect her name to Thad somehow. His middle name is Ryan, so…"

Iris cooed down at the sleeping baby, and Jamie caught a glimpse of the young mother she must have been when Adam and Krista were born. "I love it."

"Carter," Erin asked, "could you hand me my water?" She reached for a tumbler sitting on the tray on the opposite side of her hospital bed.

"Sure, love." Without warning, he moved his hand to

behind the baby's head and passed her over to Jamie. "Hold her, will you?"

Jamie gladly accepted the bundle. There was nothing like holding a baby in your arms—the sweetness, the trust from such a tiny creature to sleep so calmly in your arms. He cuddled Rayne close.

A throaty sound escaped Iris, almost a whisper, and Jamie glanced up to find an enigmatic expression on her face. "What?"

Her eyes took on a mischievous sparkle. "Good thing my uterus is no longer present."

A surprised laugh escaped him. "What does that mean?"

Iris winked. "There's nothing like watching a silver fox hold a baby to make your baby-making parts sit up and pay attention."

He had no doubt his smile took on a hungry edge. "Is that so?"

"It is," she whispered as Carter came back around the side of the bed to retrieve his child.

They stayed for a few minutes and left soon after, not wanting to tire the new parents out. Their fingers stayed securely wrapped around each other all the way to the car. Jamie opened the passenger-side door and settled Iris in, then rounded the back to the driver's side.

"Do you mind if we make a quick stop at the restaurant?" he asked, turning the key to crank the car.

"Of course not." Iris situated her seat belt, then turned slightly in her seat so that she could keep her eyes on him, something he'd noticed she did frequently in the car. "I don't have any plans tonight but to be with you."

"Sounds like my ideal plans." He reached for her hand again and brought their combined clasp to his mouth, brushed his lips lightly along the back of her hand. "I just need to check on a couple of things, and then the rest of the night is yours."

"Perfect."

They drove in an easy silence across town to the Carousel. Jamie still felt a surge of pride when he pulled into the parking lot, even fifteen years after building. His first restaurant had been a standard upscale steakhouse in a traditional brick building, but the Carousel had been his dream, and when he'd been able to make it a reality, he'd known he was exactly where he was meant to be. Now, with expansion plans in the works, that dream was growing larger, but this original location would never fail to have his heart.

He pulled the car around the back, parked near the rear entrance, and rounded the car to hand Iris out. The back portion of the restaurant was quiet this early in the day, only the kitchens buzzing with prep for their evening service. He unlocked the door to his office and ushered Iris inside. "I need to check with Francisco about an order, but I'll be right back."

She nodded. "I'll be here."

He gave her a fast, hungry kiss, then left, determined to return quickly.

His business with Francisco only took a few minutes, but when he came back to the office, it was to find Iris staring out the window, a pensive look on her face. He closed the door behind him. "Everything okay?"

She turned abruptly as if startled. "Sorry." A frown curved her mouth downward. "Just thinking."

He crossed the room slowly, studying her face. "Thinking about what?"

A wry twist took over her lips. "The last time I was in this room." A sigh left her. "I'm sorry. I don't really want to think about that night, but sometimes it sneaks up on me, you know?"

He eased up behind her, closed his arms around her waist, and pulled her back to nestle against his chest. Exactly where she belonged. "Memories do that." He knew from past experience. He settled his chin into the curve of her neck. "And hurt takes time to heal, even when good things have come into your life alongside it. Never apologize for that."

She leaned back, giving him her weight. "I'm afraid this stuff with Krista keeps bringing it back. I just want things to be normal. I want to be able to enjoy this"—she nudged him with her shoulder—"and not worry about anything else."

"Well…" He turned Iris to face him, tipped her chin up until her lips were barely a brush away from his. "I can't do anything about your daughter." He rubbed his lips over hers, savoring the softness, enjoying the scent of her as it filled his nose, the feel of her against his body. "But maybe there is something I could do about those pesky memories."

Iris's lips parted, her breath coming a hair faster, her body pushing upward to get more of his taste, his touch. "What's that?"

He continued the tantalizing tease. "I can replace bad memories of this room with good ones. After all, I want you here for a long, long time to come."

Her eyes had closed. She lifted her lids the barest amount. "What did you have in mind?"

"This."

He turned, pulling her along with him as he made his way to his desk. Walking around the back, he nudged the rolling office chair out of the way, turned, and pulled her in front of him. With a swift grasp of her waist, he lifted her easily onto the desk blotter.

"Oh!" Iris gave an uneasy chuckle, shifting her weight to settle herself in the spot. "Jamie…?"

He shook his head, settled his finger against her lips. "Don't talk." Dragged his finger along her lips. "Be very quiet."

She opened her mouth, maybe to protest, but a single tap from his finger broke off the word. Backing silently away from her, he crossed the room until he reached the door, flicked the lock, and reversed his path, his stride becoming a prowl as he approached. The shiver that took over Iris's body was crystal clear.

"I want you to lie back," he told her.

With a glance over her shoulder, Iris cleared her throat and eased her body backward until she was laid full out, stretched out for his pleasure, her head dangling from the other side of the desk.

Her trust squeezed his heart like a vise. "Now close your eyes." He paused, waiting for her to comply. When she did, he rewarded her with a single finger trailing from chin to neck to the valley between her breasts. Iris's breath caught in her throat. "Relax," he murmured. Slowly, one by one, he undid the buttons on her dress shirt, revealing inch by inch of gorgeous, creamy skin. Her breasts heaved as her breath quickened even more.

At her waist, he skipped the band of her skirt and trailed down to gorgeous knees, then reversed the journey, tangling the material of her skirt in his fist.

Iris squirmed beneath his hands. Narrowing his eyes to gauge her reaction, he gave her inner thigh a light smack. "Be still."

Iris gasped, her body instinctively arching toward his touch. "Jamie!" Shock filled the word.

Satisfaction rumbled in his chest. "Shhh."

Another firm pat to that smooth thigh. A whine left Iris's mouth. She quickly raised a hand to cover her lips.

"That's my girl."

Iris squeezed her eyes shut.

Gliding his hands down her legs, he lifted each foot and set each perky black heel onto the edge of his desk. Iris held her knees closed, but he gently pushed, making room for himself between her legs. Another smack brought a second gasp to her lips. He repeated the move on the opposite side, picking up a rhythm, alternating, first one side, then the other, turning the flesh of her inner thighs a soft blushing pink. Whimpers of pleasure left Iris with each impact, just loud enough for him to catch. "Good girl."

When her body was curving up to his touch and her murmurs became louder, he leaned over, opened her shirt fully, captured the upper edges of her bra, and pulled them down to lovingly cup each beautiful breast. "So gorgeous," he whispered against the skin of her stomach and slowly made his way up up up until he gripped one pert tip between his teeth and sucked hard.

Iris nearly came off the desk. A hard hand on her sternum pushed her back down, but he continued to suck, pulling strongly, wanting every last bit of sensation that he could give her. Wanting her taste to fill his mouth, his soul. Wanting to brand this memory, this moment on his heart forever.

"Jamie!" The grip of her hands along the sides of his head echoed the urgency coating his name. "Jamie, please!" Her pelvis rocked against him in time to the pulse of his mouth. "Please!"

A grin that felt more than a little wicked took over his mouth. He released her breast, placed a soft kiss to the tip. "Hold on for me, love."

Shit. He hadn't meant for that word to come out. But when he glanced up, Iris's eyes were closed, no hint of alarm on her face. He breathed a sigh of relief even as he circled to the other side of the desk, hands busy at the zipper of his jeans.

Iris squirmed on the desk. He stopped just behind her head. "I want you to touch yourself for me, Iris." He used his most commanding voice in case any lingering shyness made her hesitate. But she didn't. One hand slipped slowly down her stomach, caressed the skin over her mound, and snuck between her legs. He knew the minute she found her clit, startling as if she'd touched a live wire.

"That's it, beautiful." The correct endearment came easily

to his lips as he soaked in the sight before him. He freed himself from the denim. "That's it." Using one hand, he guided himself to her gasping mouth and tapped gently. The other hand went to the nearest breast. "Let me in."

Iris raised her head slightly. Her eyes opened, zeroing in on his. "Jamie?"

He smiled down at her. "Trust me."

She didn't hesitate. Her head rested back, her gaze sweeping his erection on its way past. Excitement had him harder than he ever remembered being before. When her mouth opened, he slid inside, taking it slow to give her time to adjust. Letting go of his dick, he put the hand behind her head, adjusting the angle carefully.

A groan escaped him as he slid closer to her throat. "God, Iris."

Her tongue swept the sensitive head. His erection kicked in her mouth.

And then she started sucking.

He cursed. "This is gonna be fast," he mumbled, his voice gravel.

She nodded around him.

He set up a rhythm, his gaze focusing in on her hand between her legs. "Pick up the pace. Ride that hand, Iris."

Her fingers moved faster across her clit. The sudden rocking of her pelvis up into her touch, pushing harder, chasing the high, had his own pace kicking up. It wasn't long before the point of no return loomed far too close ahead.

He pinched the hard nipple between his fingers. "Come on, beautiful."

Another pinch and a scream rose in Iris's throat, vibrating around his too-sensitive flesh, forcing him close, closer. Her hips rose off the desk. That beautiful scream surrounded his dick.

Pushed him over the edge.

Long moments later, with only the harsh sounds of their

breaths filling the small room, he withdrew from Iris's mouth. She gulped in air, eyes sealed tight, body lax across the desk. He bent to kiss her. "Okay?"

"Perfect." Panting breaths escaped even as she pushed up for more of his mouth.

He kissed her again, hard. "I think that's my line."

She grinned, eyes still closed. "We'll share; how does that sound?"

It sounded like he never wanted to let her go. "Always."

Twenty~One

Hours later, the late summer night was lit by the faint glow left from the sunset and the flash of fireflies blinking in the evening air as Jamie and Iris approached the courthouse. Seven wasn't late for the summer, but they were well on their way to August, and soon kids would be going back to school. Not long after that would be sweaters and falling leaves before Jamie began planning the holiday menus for the Carousel. It was the time of year he loved best, though he was discovering with Iris in his life, any time of year was his favorite.

Crossing the lawn that carpeted the square that formed the center of town, Jamie noticed several couples following suit, approaching the building from various angles. In a town as small as Black Wolf's Bluff, a town council meeting was the social highlight of the week. Few dared miss it.

Iris's back was tense beneath the weight of his hand, and he rubbed up and down, hoping to ease her tension. He knew the reason—Kirk—and would do anything in his power to make this easier. But some battles weren't his to fight. All he could do was stand back and provide Iris support when she looked to him for it. And dealing with her ex was definitely one of those instances—especially since putting himself within speaking distance of the prick also put him at risk of ending up in jail for punching Kirk's lights out.

He realized his grip had tightened on Iris's neck when she groaned. Immediately he eased the pressure.

Iris chuckled. "That wasn't a complaint if you didn't catch that."

He leaned down to nibble delicately, discreetly at the lobe of her ear. "I'm learning," he murmured into her skin. "Still, I have to preserve the reputation of a certain female council member that I really just want to fuck."

She shivered beneath his word, his breath, his touch. "Is that right?"

"The reputation part or the fucking part?"

"Both." She shivered again as his breath skated across her neck.

"Absolutely."

Iris's laugh was strained, the sound tinted with disappointment as he raised his head away from her.

"Mom!"

The exhale that escaped Iris's lips this time was more consternation than anything else. They both lifted their heads, watching as Krista marched toward them across the grass.

"Hey, hon," Iris called, her tone decidedly neutral. "What are you doing here tonight? You don't usually come to these meetings."

"Your question really should be, what am I doing here tonight, in front of the whole town, on the grounds of the courthouse."

It took a moment for Jamie to realize what Krista was intimating. He could practically hear Iris counting to ten in her head, but the implications got his protective instincts aroused. He was less inclined to be patient.

"Krista." He hoped his acknowledgment of the young woman would draw her attention away from her mom.

Considering the disdain in her eyes when she shifted her focus to him, he didn't think he was going to be that lucky.

"Are you trying to ruin her reputation?" Krista asked.

Jamie felt the leash he held on his patience give way. "I thought I was doing a damn good job of exactly that."

"Well you were wrong."

"Krista, stop." Iris frowned at her daughter, and Jamie felt like she was searching her daughter's face, either for an answer to why she was acting this way, or a solution. "We weren't doing anything wr—"

"You were kissing right here, out in front of everyone."

"So?" A summer breeze blew Iris's bangs into her eyes, and she pushed them back, shaking her head. "There's nothing scandalous about kissing."

"People will believe—"

Iris stiffened. "Believe what?"

Krista hesitated, then seemed to gather her courage. "They'll believe you are...loose...just like Daddy said."

Iris gasped, the sound holding a world of pain and disbelief.

Jamie stepped between her and Krista, blocking out her daughter, blocking out the world. Iris latched on to his shirt with both fists, her devastated gaze rising to meet his, silently begging him to tell her Krista hadn't said the words. But she had. He knew she'd been aware of the statements Kirk had made around town, but to hear them parroted from her daughter... He felt a tick start up in his jaw. Cupping Iris's cheek, he held her stare. "Would you excuse us for a moment?" He leaned in, brushed a kiss across her lips in what he hoped was reassurance. "I'll be right behind you, don't worry."

Iris opened her mouth, maybe to protest, maybe not, then closed it abruptly. "I'll see you inside." She barely brushed her glance over Krista as she passed.

Krista watched her mom go, protest in her eyes. "Mom!"

When she would've followed Iris, Jamie casually took her elbow, being certain to keep his grip open and easy. He had no intention of hurting the girl, but he was done with her hurting Iris.

"We need to talk."

Krista whirled back to face him. "We have nothing to talk about. You don't belong in our lives."

"Not in yours, but when it comes to your mom, that's where you're wrong." He dropped his hand, narrowing his gaze on Krista's pouting face. "Your mother has accepted me into her life. I do belong there. I hope to belong there for a very long time. You, on the other hand, are running the risk of being pushed away if you keep this up."

Anger twisted Krista's mouth. "What do you know about it?"

"I know you're causing her pain. If you'd open your eyes and really look, you'd see it too."

Krista shook her head. "You don't really know her. You met, what, a couple months ago? You don't know our family."

"I don't know you because you won't give me the chance," Jamie corrected. "But I do know Iris, and I know her heart breaks a little bit more every time you do this. I also know I'll do anything to stand between her and what's hurting her. Right now, that's you."

Krista stuttered. "You don't— How could you—"

Jamie sighed. "Krista…look. You're an adult. You've been in relationships before. Just because your mom is older, just because she is a parent does not mean that Iris doesn't deserve the exact same things in her life that you want in yours. Acting like a spoiled little girl who isn't getting the attention she wants doesn't change that.

"She deserves to be happy. I hope I make her happy; she says I do. The only thing making her unhappy right now is your attitude." He deliberately softened his voice. "I know you're afraid of losing her. Believe me, I have no desire to separate her from you or from Adam. She loves you both, and she wants you in her life. I would never stand in the way of that."

"But you just said—"

He held up a hand. "I said you're hurting her. And yes, if you hurt her, I'll defend her. But it doesn't have to be that way. Just get to know me. Give me a chance. Give your mother a chance to be happy. She deserves that most of all."

For a moment he thought the anger in her eyes wavered, thought maybe he was getting through to her. But the emotion solidified once again even as tears dripped down her cheeks. "You have no idea what you're talking about. Just leave us alone!"

Before he could get out another word, Krista spun away from him, marching across the grass. She stumbled, righted herself, and continued on, but that single moment sparked concern in Jamie's chest. Iris would never forgive him if something happened to her daughter. He would never forgive himself.

Not wanting to give her further reason for anger, he kept a discreet distance behind her but followed carefully to be certain Krista made it to her car safely. The young woman hurried toward the southeast end of the square, the corner where the pub sat just off the main road. Parking was limited on meeting nights, the few spaces diagonally situated around the square all full, with the areas lining each road that stuck out like spokes on a wagon wheel equally packed. Krista must have parked in the lot on the opposite side of the Drunken Otter.

Streetlights illuminated the sidewalk as he followed Krista's progress. He lost sight of her as she rounded the corner of the pub, and he hurried to catch up. When he reached the corner, he slowed, peered around the brick edge

—and caught sight of Krista, several feet into the parking lot, a large figure looming in front of her.

Kirk.

Jamie cursed under his breath.

"What's going on, baby girl? Why are you crying?"

Jamie wished the concern in Kirk's voice sounded genuine, but he doubted too much. The man didn't seem to give two licks about his family, so what was he doing now, here, with Krista? Maybe Jamie was wrong and the man really did care about his daughter more than himself.

Maybe.

Krista's tears had turned into full-on weeping. "Mom…" She shook her head, choking on her sobs.

Kirk opened his arms, and Krista walked into them. Jamie straightened, prepared to walk away, until he heard the words…

"Your mother doesn't deserve your tears."

What the hell? What was Kirk saying?

"But she…" The rest of Krista's words were muffled against Kirk's chest, unable to reach Jamie where he stood.

Kirk patted Krista's back, but there was something about the gleam in the man's eye, evident even in the dusk, that didn't reflect paternal concern. "Can't you see, Krista? She's just playing the whore with that man."

Krista jerked backward out of her father's arms. "What?"

Maybe sensing that he'd gone a step too far, Kirk sputtered. "Her focus should be on you, baby girl, not some rich guy trying to horn in on our family."

"But…" Krista shook her head. "She's not— Mom wouldn't—" Tears thickened her words. "Mom's not like that."

Kirk rubbed his thumbs over his daughter's cheeks. "She is like that. Why do you think I had to leave? Don't you remember the Halloween costume? A saloon girl, of all things. Showing herself to every man that walked by."

"It was just a dress," Krista whispered.

Anger flashed in Kirk's eyes, and Krista took another step back. "It wasn't just a dress. You know that!"

Jamie tensed, ready to step in whether Krista would want him to or not.

"Mom's not like that." The words were firmer, more sure this time. "She's a good mom."

"She's a terrible wife." Kirk's fists clenched at his sides, clear in the glow from the nearby streetlight. "Look what she did to our family."

"What you did," Krista said. "You wanted—"

So Krista did know about that. Before she could finish her sentence, Kirk interrupted with a harsh laugh. "Do you really believe that? Do you really believe I would even bring that up to my wife?" He slapped his chest. "Do I seem like that kind of guy, Krista?"

She hesitated, shook her head. "N-no," she stuttered. "No, of course not."

"No," Kirk repeated. "I'm not. Whatever stories your mom spun up, they were likely to give her an excuse to go be with that guy."

Jamie grimaced in disgust. Now he knew where Krista was getting fed all these ideas. What she believed about him didn't matter, but if she could believe these lies about her mom... Disappointment weighed heavy on his chest, more so because he knew exactly what this would do to Iris, and he had to tell her. He had no choice. He wouldn't keep secrets.

One final look assured him that Krista was safe in the parking lot with her father. He turned, leaving the two of them alone. The whole way back to the courthouse, he wondered what he would say to Iris. How could he explain what he'd seen, what he now knew: that it wasn't just Krista she was fighting against. Kirk had his hand in this, and that was going to make the fight so much harder moving forward.

Twenty~Two

I ris tried to focus on the music blasting across the dance floor of the Drunken Otter. Lily and JD were doing a two-step nearby, with Claire and a few others joining in. But Iris found she couldn't concentrate enough to make the steps come together. Giving a laughing Jamie a pat to his chest, she murmured a need to visit the restroom and left the dance floor.

She should've known her exit would be noticed. She hadn't been inside the restroom more than two minutes before Lily and Claire followed suit.

"Hey, girl!" Claire said. "What's going on?"

"We can tell you're troubled, Iris," Lily said. "You know you can talk to us. What's got you upset?"

Iris turned from the mirror with a heavy sigh. Leaning back against the countertop, she crossed her arms over her chest. "It's Krista."

Lily and Claire exchanged a knowing glance.

Iris took a moment to explain what had happened before the council meeting the other night, as well as what Jamie had explained to her about his talk with Krista and following her to her car shortly after. Her friends nodded along, murmuring sympathetic sounds as the story unfolded.

"Wow." Claire gave Iris a sympathetic smile. "It looks like she's a little more entrenched than you'd hoped."

"I know you were thinking maybe things were getting better," Lily added.

"I was hoping." She pushed her bangs back from her face. "I mean, at least we've gone from her pitching a fit in front of my apartment to a whole day at Jamie's without an outright explosion. It seemed like a sign of progress. But this..." Iris felt tears burn the backs of her eyes. "I just don't know how to get through to her." She blinked hard. "Not that it's gonna stop me from dating Jamie, but it's hard knowing your child doesn't approve."

"Not to mention having her follow you around town, judging you for the least show of affection," Lily said.

"Exactly." Iris turned back to the sink, started the cool water, and gathered some in her cupped hands before splashing her face, hoping the shock of the temperature would push back her tears. She braced her palms on either side of the sink and stared at her friends in the mirror. "It's the only thing marring this time with Jamie, and I really want to enjoy it. I don't want this cloud hanging over me."

"I wish there was some way we could help," Claire said.

"I do too," Iris agreed, "but like I told Adam, this is up to Krista. If she doesn't want to change her attitude, no one can force her."

"But you can limit how much she is allowed to affect you," Lily pointed out, always the voice of reason. "Boundaries are good for anyone, but especially for someone causing you this much heartache."

"I'm afraid I'm about to be pushed to that point," Iris said.

Or maybe already had been. She knew she couldn't allow Krista to keep doing this, but the idea of distancing herself from her daughter was an arrow to her heart. And it wasn't just about having Jamie in her life—she wanted him in her life, but this was also about Krista allowing Iris to make her own decisions without judgment. Her daughter refused to listen, and that meant in the very near future Iris would be forced to limit contact in order to have the freedom and the calm that she wanted in her life right now.

Back at their table, the men were joking and toasting each other with wings that, from the steam rising from them, had apparently just arrived at the table. Iris took her seat next to Jamie. He turned to wrap an arm around her shoulder.

Leaning in, he nuzzled her neck. "Are you okay?"

The soft words had that tingle returning to the backs of her eyes. "Not really."

Jamie eased back until their eyes met. "Do you want to go?"

"No." She shook her head. "No, I don't want to ruin the night."

"I don't have to spend the night at the pub for it not to be ruined." He ran a thumb along her cheekbone. "Anytime I'm with you, that's a win."

She looked deep into those green, green eyes and saw honesty there. "Okay. I'd really like to go. I need some quiet time with you."

The words *with you* brought a flare of gold to his eyes. "I am more than happy to arrange that."

Jamie excused himself and went up to the bar to pay their tab. He came back a few minutes later with a to-go order of wings. "Dinner for the road." His grin was hungry, for wings or that alone time she'd mentioned, she wasn't certain, but she knew which one would be better to distract her. "Ready?"

"Yes." Relief filled her as she stood up from the table. "I enjoyed seeing you guys."

"You take care, Iris," Claire said.

"Call us if you need us," Lily added. Iris nodded and

entwined her fingers with Jamie's, allowing him to lead her out the door.

The parking lot of the Drunken Otter was half light, half shadow by this time of the night. Jamie had parked in a corner, and now he escorted her to his car with sure steps.

Iris breathed deeply, taking in the summer air, focused in on Jamie's fingers entangled with hers, his steady breath as he walked beside her, the scent of his cologne filling her lungs. And with each step she added another brick to the wall between the worries in her mind and thoughts of her lover. As they rounded the car toward the passenger side, she used their grip to tug him to a stop. "Jamie."

His name on her lips was husky, the two syllables filled with need. She could hear it, and knew he could as well by the narrowing of his eyes, his gaze sweeping over her face. "What do you need, beautiful?"

"I need you," she said softly. "I need you to take my mind off all of this. Please," she softly begged.

Jamie's mouth firmed as he stared down at her. "Anything you want," he promised.

He dropped her hand, and his fingers filtered into her hair as he gripped the sides of her head. One step, two and her back met the car door. A hoarse rumble left his mouth as it descended on hers.

He tasted so good, like honey and beer and warm male. She opened to the thrust of his tongue, letting him fill her, letting him take complete control. Thoughts of Krista dissipated; sadness retreated into the background. Iris gave herself over to Jamie's touch, losing all sense of time and place.

A truck passing along the road, its exhaust an obnoxiously loud roar, brought both of them back to awareness. Jamie eased his body away from hers. "Let's take this inside," he said roughly.

She wasn't sure what he had in mind, but she prayed to God he meant someplace closer than her apartment. She didn't wanna lose the closeness she'd just found for a thirty-minute drive.

Apparently Jamie didn't either, because he reached for her the second he slid into the driver's seat. His groan as their lips met sent tingles down her spine. She shifted in her seat, pushing her body to face him, ignoring the console between them to reach for him. The buttons on his shirt gave way easily, and as he devoured her, she sought out the naked skin beneath, the heat of his body, the crinkle of hair beneath her fingers. All male, all good. He felt so good. Sharing touch always felt good, but with Jamie, it was…special. She craved it. She wanted him with an intensity she'd never experienced before—and reveled in the experience every second.

When one of her nails scraped across Jamie's nipple, he threw his head back. "God." Hard hands slid down the sides of her throat, along her shoulders, down to her breasts. He cupped her, kneading on top of her clothing. "Iris."

"Hmmm?" The pleasure taking over his face had her squirming in her seat. Heat gathered in her core. Her nipples. "I want you, Jamie. Now."

The growl that left him at her words thrilled her. He reached down and pushed the button to slide his seat back. "Come here, beautiful."

She dragged the flowing folds of her skirt up to her hips, thankful for the darkness as she climbed over the console and onto Jamie's lap. He tilted the steering wheel up, giving her a few extra inches of room as she settled into place. The back of Jamie's seat lowered with another push of a button, allowing him to recline, and he hunched down in the seat to bring their pelvises into alignment. The hard ridge of his body between her legs drew a whimper to her lips.

Jamie's laugh held strain. "How's that, beautiful?"

Perfect. One hand went to the ridge rising between the two windows, the other twisting in the shoulder of his shirt. "That's perfect."

She refused to think about anything but him. The windows were already fogging, but even if they weren't, the two of them were well-hidden by the darkness at the edges of the parking lot. Even Jamie's hands, sliding up from the hem of her shirt, couldn't be seen as they reached her bra and pulled roughly at the cups. "Gimme," he demanded.

She arched her back. Hard nipples met his fingertips, scraped across the rough skin. A shiver shook her hard.

Jamie pinched lightly at the tips. His hips took up a rocking rhythm that dragged his tight erection against the most sensitive part of her body. A hiss left him.

Iris reached for his belt buckle. It was her turn to demand what she wanted, and his body was it. The leather gave way to her fingers, allowing her to grip the button beneath and twist. A careful tug of the zipper rasped the steel teeth down his body.

"Are you sure, beautiful?" He drew her nipples away from her body, creating a tension that had her sucking in a breath. "I can get you off—we don't have to do this."

"Oh yes we do." She dug beneath the layers of cloth until hot skin met her touch. "We most definitely do."

One last look around told her the windows were opaque. She rose up on her knees, pulled her panties to one side, and angled his erection toward her opening. The sweet slide of him into her body was everything she wanted and needed at that moment.

Climax took her immediately.

"Fuck!" Jamie went rigid beneath her, his breaths deep and hard as he held himself there for her pleasure. Long moments later, when her contractions eased, he released his death grip on her hips.

Iris collapsed onto his chest. "Sorry," she mumbled.

"Oh, we're not done."

She lifted her head to search out his gaze in the dark. "No? The jerk of his head was definitive. "No." And with gentle touches, hard rubs, nips and licks and kisses, he brought her back up until they were both at the peak, frantically chasing the high they both needed. The touch of Jamie's thumb against her aching clit set her off; her rhythmic squeezes sent him over the edge.

Breathy laughter filled the car as they both came back to the world. "Not what I expected," Jamie admitted against her hair, "but I'd do it all over again if someone would let me."

"Talk to your other half," Iris murmured, exhaustion closing in. "I think he might have something to say about that."

"No doubt." He brushed back her hair and placed a kiss on her forehead. "Let's go find someplace more comfortable to snuggle."

"Okay." She rolled off him, dragging her skirt down as she settled into her seat. Jamie straightened himself, cranked the car, and pointed them toward her apartment. Instead of worries filling Iris's thoughts, it was memories of the past few minutes and dreams of the moments to come. Much sweeter, and Iris hoped to keep things that way for a little bit longer.

Twenty~Three

The Carousel glittered like crown jewels set atop its own lake. Iris admired the view of the glass-enclosed building, now blazing with lights, as she pulled into the parking lot and found a space along the periphery. The lot was full—of course it would be on a busy Friday night—but she knew Jamie had arranged to take a few hours off to have dinner with her family. Adam and Chloe, and hopefully Krista, would all be here soon.

The pier leading from the parking lot to the double glass doors that formed the entry to the restaurant's second floor was dotted with couples and groups waiting for their tables to be ready. She made her way through the crowd, her gaze repeatedly seeking out the man-made lake beyond the building. Jamie had certainly built a destination when he'd built the Carousel. Even with her memories of what had happened here with Kirk, she couldn't be blinded to the beauty of what Jamie had created.

Just inside the entry stood a slim glass podium, behind which waited a young man, sharply dressed in black and white, that she didn't recognize. His name tag read, *Sam*.

"Good evening, ma'am. May I have your name, please?"

She gave him a warm smile. "Yes, Iris Daniels."

"Ah, yes. Mr. Worthington's guests." He set down the pen in his hand and raised a finger. "Wait here just one moment."

Iris watched him cross the restaurant toward the back hall where Jamie's office was located. She'd gotten caught up in searching out her favorite part of the décor, the carousel horses adorning the walls between the wide windows, when she sensed Jamie's approach. His energy was too strong to miss, even in this crowd. He wore a crisp white shirt that set off the deep tan of his neck from hours in the sun, and long black slacks emphasized his height. He always made her feel tiny in comparison even though she was average height for a woman, not only because of his height but because of that heavy barrel chest and the heft of his muscles. Just looking at him move gave her the shivers.

His smile lit a glow inside her. "There you are, beautiful."

A thrill went through her. Jamie's hand enveloped hers, and in front of everyone in the dining room, he drew her closer, leaned down, and pressed his lips to hers. When he drew back, she was breathless. "You look wonderful tonight."

She glanced down at the copper-colored sheath she wore. "I wanted to dress up for the evening."

"And give me a gorgeous gift, because I get to look at you all night."

A blush heated her cheeks. "Are you flirting with me?"

He winked. "Every chance I get."

Her heart fluttered into her throat, her smile so wide her mouth ached. "You make me feel so special, Jamie," she said, the words bubbling up without warning.

"Good." He eased in for another kiss. "That's exactly what I was hoping for."

"Stop groping my mom," Adam said somewhere behind her.

Iris sputtered out a laugh. "Adam!"

"Never," Jamie said, winking at her son this time. Moving

to Iris's side to face the newcomers, he reached for Chloe. "Nice to see you again, Chloe." When he kissed the back of her hand, Adam gave a mock growl.

A masculine chuckle sounded behind Adam's back, and Michael appeared to one side of him. "Just ignore him," Michael said to Adam. "He can't seem to stop himself."

Jamie chuckled. "Keep it up, son. Do you guys want dinner tonight or should I leave you out in the cold?"

"It's not cold; it's hot." Adam tugged at his collar. "I think you're in the wrong season, mate. Must be the age creeping up on you."

Jamie turned back to Iris, a huge sigh leaving him as he rolled his eyes. "Rescue me from these two?"

Iris laughed, shaking her head. "You're on your own."

The boys chuckled.

Jamie escorted them to a table at the end of the dining room overlooking the lake. Set atop a dais, much like the one she'd shared with her ex-husband all those months ago, this table was massive, suited for a large party. Candelabras adorned the center, their candlelight shining off the gold of the tableware and the soft petals of the flowers gracing the length of the table. The entire setup was much more elaborate than the normal decor for the tables in the Carousel.

"Jamie!" Iris stroked the edge of a set of gold-rimmed dishes. "This is lovely."

"Only the best for my girl," Jamie told her.

As they settled into their seats, Iris glanced around, anxiety starting a flutter in her stomach. "Krista's not here yet," she murmured quietly to Jamie.

He gave her hand a squeeze as he took the seat next to her. "Give her time. I'm choosing to believe in her."

She met his eyes, absorbing the calm reassurance she found there. This man who'd been treated with nothing but disdain and outright hostility from her daughter was choosing to give her grace; the least Iris could do was the same. "I will too."

Jamie explained to them all that he'd ordered a special menu for tonight, being certain to first check with Iris to make sure everyone would enjoy what he'd selected. Toward the end of his little speech, Iris heard loud noises from the area of the front podium. Shouting. She squinted in that direction, seeing a large figure yelling at the young man, Sam, who had spoken to them earlier. Iris couldn't see clearly who it was, but Adam's, "Is that Dad?" told her everything she needed to know.

What was her ex-husband doing here?

Somehow Iris was on her feet. Jamie cursed beside her, and she heard the click of his phone, presumably to dial someone—maybe the cops? At the same time she noticed Krista next to her father, the panicked look on her face shooting alarm through Iris. Krista caught sight of her and hurried across the dining room just as Iris heard Jamie speaking into his cell.

"Francisco, get Brian into the dining room now."

Not the cops, then. Should she be relieved her ex wasn't about to be arrested in front of their children?

Unfortunately Krista wasn't the only one who'd seen them across the wide dining room. Kirk had as well. Pushing past the podium, he followed in his daughter's footsteps, charging in their direction, rage clear on his face. Iris caught her breath. From the corner of her eye she saw Adam stand, saw him place a firm hand on Chloe's shoulder to keep her in her seat where she would be more protected. There was little doubt that was what was uppermost in her son's mind as he watched his father race toward them—it was on Iris's as well. And when Jamie stood, one arm coming in front of her to push her back a couple of steps, she knew he felt it too. Protected behind his shoulder, she watched with increasing horror as Krista and Kirk approached the table.

Tears fell in a torrent down Krista's face. She was dressed as if she'd been coming for their dinner, her glittery shirt and pressed slacks clear evidence of her intent, but words soaked in sobs spilled from her lips. "Mom, I didn't... I'm sorry. I tried to stop him. H-he's drunk, he doesn't— Don't..."

Kirk shoved their daughter out of his way as he reached them. Thank God for Michael, who caught Krista before she hit the floor. Iris cried out, the sound half fear, half anger. "Kirk!"

Her ex-husband slammed into the opposite side of the table from them, the smell of alcohol continuing across the space until it filled Iris's nostrils. "There you are, bitch!"

Shock jolted through her.

"Kirk—"

That was Jamie. Iris wanted to tell him to stop, to not draw attention to himself. She didn't want anyone hurt, and though a part of her would never have believed Kirk would do such a thing, she had to admit she didn't know the man standing in front of her now. Maybe she never had.

"You!" Kirk jabbed a finger at Jamie. "You fucked my wife."

"What?" Iris spluttered.

Kirk was fixated on Jamie now, ignoring her. "That's why she left, ain't it? Because you broke up our family. You took her away from me!"

She couldn't let him do this. "You did that just fine on your own, Kirk. You have no one to blame but yourself."

"Stay out of this," Kirk spat at her.

"I won't stay out of it." She fisted her hands, willing them to stop shaking. "It's my life and my boyfriend and you are not wanted here. You need to leave." Beside her she could hear Jamie murmuring to someone, presumably on his phone, to call the cops.

"I'm not leaving until he admits that he broke up our family."

"He didn't, Kirk." Anger blazed in her chest, drowning out the fear. "You did."

"Shut up, whore!"

"Dad!" Horror filled Krista's eyes, spilling into the tears dripping down her face as she stood in the protective circle of Michael's arms.

Adam's fury was a palpable aura around her son. He left his spot to round the table, just escaping Iris's frantic attempt to hold him back. "You're leaving, Dad." He reached for Kirk's arm.

Staggering back, Kirk threw an unsteady punch. Thank God it missed its mark, sailing futilely through the air. The momentum tipped Kirk off balance, and he fell to his knees.

Adam stood, staring down at his father. The look in his eyes, in both her children's eyes, broke Iris's heart.

"Dad," her son said, his voice full of warning, "there's no one to blame for all of this but yourself. Not Mom, not us kids, just you. This is what you wanted, and you got it."

Kirk blinked up at him blindly.

Krista cleared her throat and stepped carefully away from Michael, staying outside of Kirk's reach. "Adam's right, Dad."

A jolt of shock shot through Iris.

"Mom told us what happened," Krista continued, not looking at Iris. "She told us that you wanted to open your marriage. You wanted to sleep with other women."

Krik's mouth twisted angrily. "That's a damn lie."

"No, it's not," Jamie said. "I heard you, right over there"—he pointed across the dining room, ignoring the audience Kirk had drawn—"that very night. That's what you wanted, what you asked of your wife, and now you have to live with the consequences."

"I believe Mom," Krista said. "And you know who else I believe?" She pointed to Jamie. "Him. Because he's been better to Mom than you ever were the last few years. I've watched it with my own eyes, and I haven't wanted to believe it because I wanted our family back together, but it's true. He loves her, in a way that you don't anymore. So no, you don't get to come in here and ruin our night."

Kirk deflated, all the anger and spite giving way to defeat if the slump of his body told Iris's anything. She breathed a sigh of relief.

A commotion across the dining room had Iris glancing over. Cops appeared at the front door. Adam saw them too, as well as two men lingering close to the dais—Francisco and Brian, Iris assumed. "Let's go, Dad," he said.

As Adam pulled on his arm to get him off the floor, Kirk stumbled. Michael stepped forward and grabbed Kirk's other arm, looping it over his shoulder to mimic Adam, and they escorted Kirk's swaying, stumbling body back to the front door.

Jamie silently left Iris's side, leaving her feeling cold as he moved around the table to stand at the front of the dais and address the dining room. "I apologize," he said loudly, clearly, "to all of you for the interruption to your meal. Please forgive us, and continue to have a good time. Dessert is on the house tonight."

A smattering of applause came from across the dining area. Jamie turned and rounded the table, gesturing for all of them to sit back down.

"Are you all right, beautiful?" He gathered her against his chest, practically pulling her into his seat to get her close enough to comfort. She tucked her face into his neck and nodded without verbally responding. Warmth seeped in to take the place of the chill holding her body captive.

"Mom?" The word was tentative, shaking, as if Krista was afraid her mother wouldn't acknowledge her. Iris wondered for the briefest moment if she should, but she couldn't leave her daughter hanging out to dry. With a sigh she turned her

ELLA SHERIDAN

face the slightest bit, still keeping contact with Jamie's skin, to meet her daughter's eyes.

"I'm so sorry." Krista's gaze flitted to Jamie, then back to Iris. "I'm sorry for the way I've acted. I understand now." She stopped to wipe fresh tears from her cheeks. "I was looking for things to go back to the way they were, but they can't, not after what Dad put you through. I won't keep standing in the way of you being happy. You deserve it." She faced Jamie squarely. "You make her happy. Thank you."

Jamie's grin was only half-formed. "I hadn't expected the first time your mother hears that I love her to be from her daughter."

Iris's eyes went wide. Krista had said that, hadn't she? And Jamie wasn't denying it.

Krista gave a hiccuping laugh. "Sorry about that."

Jamie's grin appeared fully this time. "Oh, don't worry. I intend to talk to her about it again later."

"Well"—Krista wiped at her face again, her smile watery —"good luck with that."

"I'm right here, you know." And yes, she sounded cranky, but good grief, they were talking about her, after all.

Jamie and Krista both laughed, and in that moment Iris caught a glimpse of a future she had doubted could ever exist.

When Adam and Michael returned, Iris stood and walked over to her son. Gripping his broad shoulders, she pulled him in for a tight hug. "Are you all right?"

"I think we are all, all right now." He returned her hug for a long moment, then moved to sit next to Chloe and took her hand, giving her a comforting kiss.

Iris turned to Michael. "I can't thank you enough for your help."

"It's what we do for our friends," Michael said and reached down to place a small peck on her cheek. "Thanks for making my dad happy," he whispered for only her to hear.

Iris's tears returned, but she fought them down as she walked back to her seat. The waitstaff approached the table and quietly began to take drink orders. She leaned close and whispered to Jamie, "So do we have a chat planned for later?"

Jamie winked. "A chat...and more."

Her laughter was genuine this time, tears disappearing beneath the sweetness of the moment.

Twenty-Four

"That is not how I expected this night to go." Iris breathed deep of the night air, eyes on the stars twinkling in the sky as Jamie walked her to her car.

His warm hand rubbed up and down her back. "Me neither."

She hesitated. "What will happen to him?" She didn't want to care, but she'd spent a lifetime caring what happened to Kirk. If she was honest, though, that wasn't what concerned her now. What concerned her was how what happened to him would affect her children.

Jamie sighed. "Hopefully he'll spend the night in the drunk tank and be let out in the morning. I called Ronnie."

Iris literally skidded to a stop. "The police chief?"

Jamie pulled her close to his side, bringing their hips together, and restarted their walk. "Yes." He squeezed her gently. "Hopefully this will be a wake-up call for Kirk to get himself together."

One could only hope. Still, it blew her mind that Jamie would intervene on behalf of her ex.

Maybe he was thinking of her kids as much as she was.

They reached her car, and Jamie placed a kiss on her forehead. "Meet you at the apartment?"

They'd spent more time at his house, but tonight she wanted—no, needed—complete privacy. No Michael wandering in and out, no housekeeper showing up in the morning. She loved that Jamie had a good support system, but she needed him to herself for a while.

"Definitely."

Jamie kissed her lips this time. "Be careful driving."

"I will."

Jamie had told her he needed to close out a few things, but Francisco would take care of the rest. He'd be a half hour or so behind her. When she got to the apartment, she climbed the steps with legs that felt like lead and realized the reality of everything that had happened that night was finally hitting her. Inside, she left the lights off and absorbed the quiet of the peaceful home she'd built for herself as she left a trail of clothes on her way to the bathroom. The water gushed from the faucet when she turned it on to heat. Taking off her makeup took no more than a minute, and then she was sliding into the slowly rising water as it steamed up the bathroom.

Whirling thoughts shouted at her from all corners of her brain, but Iris sank deeper into the water and let the heat and humidity gradually wipe everything else out.

That's where Jamie found her when he arrived, half asleep in the bathtub. She murmured drowsily at the sight of him in the doorway. "I knew there was a good reason I gave you a key to my apartment," she said, a smirk waking up her face.

"Not having to get out of the hot bath?"

"Of course." With her toes she reached up and flipped the plug open to allow some of the cooling water to drain. Jamie reached down and turned on the faucet to refill the hot water.

He winked in her direction. "We make a good team."

"We do." She narrowed her eyes on him as he began to unbutton his shirt. "Which reminds me…"

His shirt fell open, revealing the wide expanse of his chest. Her fingers itched to travel through the hair that raced down the center to his slacks.

Jamie dropped his shirt on the floor. "Reminds you…?"

His fingers went to his zipper, and every thought but seeing him naked fled her brain. "Gimme a minute."

His gaze was indulgent. And sinful. He unzipped his pants, which dropped to the bathroom floor to join his button-down. Tight black boxers cupped him lovingly, just like she wanted to.

"Off."

He cocked a brow at her but complied. Boxers and socks landed on the rest of the pile. Jamie moved toward the tub.

"Stop."

The slow rise of his cock told her he wasn't bothered by her demands. "Was there something you wanted?" he asked, the words gravel-rough.

"Just to look at you."

His shaft hit full mast. He leaned a shoulder against the tile wall and waited, giving her full rein to look.

After a long moment, Iris sighed. "You're beautiful."

Jamie huffed a laugh and climbed into the opposite end of the too-small tub from her. "Women are beautiful." Gripping her feet, he pulled each up until they lay across his thighs, which he settled on the outsides of her legs.

"I know what I'm talking about," she protested.

Jamie didn't object further. "Where were we a minute ago?"

She squirmed.

"Oh yes." He took each foot in hand and began a hard massage of her arches that had her eyes rolling back in her head. "You said, that reminds me…"

She allowed her body to slide down until her chin was at

the level of the water. Jamie reached behind him and turned off the water, then speared her with his green gaze. "You were saying?"

She gathered her courage. "What was that Krista said to her father about you?" Not that she didn't know. She knew very well what words had left Krista's mouth, but somehow she couldn't bring herself to say them out loud.

Jamie's amusement said he knew exactly which words she was talking about and why she hadn't voiced them. "Do you mean about you being happy?"

She jerked one foot away and used her toes again, this time to flick water at Jamie. "That is not what I meant." He was enjoying making this harder for her.

"Hmmm..." He recaptured her foot and rubbed the center pad until she moaned. "What could it have been?"

"Jamie," she warned.

Chuckling, he brought one foot to his mouth and scraped his teeth over her big toe. A shiver shot through her.

"Close your eyes," he said softly.

She could feel the vee between her brows as she digested his words. Why did he want her eyes closed? Staring into her eyes, she thought she detected a hint of vulnerability in this man she could have sworn was never vulnerable.

Her response was as soft as his. "Okay."

When her eyes were closed, he said, the words again as soft as a breeze, "I believe she said I love you."

Iris kept her eyes closed, not wanting to spoil the moment. Not wanting to open her eyes and see that Jamie was full of regret or ready to dial back his words. Well, Krista's words, to be precise. Still...

"I think that's what she said.," she agreed. "But"—gulp —"I don't think she meant *herself*."

"No." He took each of her toes, rubbing them between his fingers. Iris moaned. "I don't think it was Krista that she was talking about."

173

Impatience overcame her trepidation. Iris squinted her eyes open to glare at the man in her bathtub. "So what did she mean?" she asked pointedly.

Jamie's eyes were tender as he gazed at her across the water. "She was saying that I"—he lifted a hand and pointed at himself—"love you"—the same fingers pointed toward Iris —"and she was right."

Iris gasped. The movement had her sliding along the bottom of the tub, and her head dipped beneath the water. She came up sputtering. Long moments passed as she got herself back together.

Finally she had to ask, "Was she?"

Jamie moved to massaging her calves. "She was." He shrugged. "I would've told you myself, but she beat me to it." His grin was wicked.

Something tight and aching in Iris's chest loosened, allowing her to breathe again. Jamie loved her. Somehow that knowledge didn't feel new; she felt like she had known it for a long time, in fact. No man would be as patient as he had been with her if he wasn't in love. And if she was honest with herself, she knew beyond a doubt that Jamie was one in a million. A man worthy of her trust. A man who understood her background and her trauma and her quirks and loved her anyway, loved her enough to walk with her through them instead of abandoning her to them. And she also knew, beyond any doubt, that...

"I love you too."

Jamie's head fell back against the bathroom tile, and he let out a hearty roar of laughter. Iris felt her eyes nearly bug out. "What is that?"

It took time to get himself back under control, but when he finally did, he gripped her knees hard. "That's relief, beautiful."

"Wait. You...doubting?" She shook her head. "I don't believe it."

"Believe it." He sat up, trailing his hands from her knees along her inner thighs, closer and closer to where she wanted him to touch most. "Remember what I told Adam? There's not a man alive who doesn't get nervous when he's waiting for his girl to say yes."

"You are not asking me to marry you," Iris said, the words nearly choked off by her closing throat.

"No, I'm not." His palm met her mound, turned, cupped her. One finger found her clit and lightly began to tease. "But knowing you like I do, this may be as close as I ever get to a proposal. And," he said forcefully, staving off the objection that rose to her lips, "I'm perfectly fine with that in my future."

She relaxed back into the water.

"But I needed to know…" He slid one thick finger down, found her entrance, and entered her, pushing deep. "I needed to know you were mine."

Iris's back curved instinctively, and she spread her legs as wide as the tub would allow, giving Jamie all the access he wanted. "I'm definitely yours, Jamie."

"Good, beautiful." He began a slow out-and-in motion that set her nerves tingling. "Don't forget it."

Her chuckle was more breath than actual sound. "I don't think I can."

Jamie added another finger. "Now, on to more important things."

She forced herself to focus on his words even as she tilted her pelvis to meet his thrust. "More important than saying 'I love you'?"

"Definitely more important." He picked up the pace. "Let me rock you to sleep."

He was rocking something, all right. She closed her eyes, breathed in his scent, his presence, and let go.

Epilogue

T*hree months later*

FALL LEAVES DRIFTED DOWN from the forest of trees over their heads, showering Jamie and Iris in a cascade of oranges and yellows and browns as they made their way through the resort grounds to the massive cobblestone patio designed as an outdoor event space around one side of the main building. Black Wolf Resort had opened to much fanfare nearly a month ago, and was booked solid for the next year already. Erin's crews were hard at work completing the remaining two main buildings before they began construction on a series of cabins dotted among the property. Iris took in the gorgeous space, now crowded with Erin's and Carter's closest friends and their families, officials from town, and locals who had known Erin since she was a little girl—all here to celebrate the arrival of Erin and Carter's precious family addition.

The official celebration in Black Wolf's Bluff had been held off until Thad could be included. Though Carter's family held a baby shower in New York, only now could Thad get away for the fall break from school to spend a week at the resort. Erin and Carter stood to one side of the courtyard with their son, little Rayne held securely in Erin's arms, to welcome the town and introduce their new baby to those who hadn't met her.

When they approached, Carter reached across Thad to pull Jamie into a bro hug. "Thanks for showing up."

"Of course." Jamie slapped the man on the back, then reached down to shake Thad's hand. "We wouldn't miss it. It's too important."

"We're welcoming Baby Rayne," Thad said.

"That's exactly what we're doing," Iris agreed, reaching to give the little boy a hug. The scent of candy and little boy wrapped around her heart. "And celebrating your family. That's so special. Congratulations, Thad."

The eleven-year-old beamed. "She's named after me."

Erin's look was just as proud as Thad's. "And we wouldn't have it any other way, hon." She patted the pink-blanket-enfolded bundle in her arms on the butt. "There's no one else Rayne would rather be named after."

A small, fussy whimper came from within the blanket. Thad immediately perked his head up. "Does she need a change?"

Carter leaned over, his sure fingers pulling back the blanket to reveal a full head of black hair on the sweetest face Iris had seen in a long, long time. A face that reminded her distinctly of Thad. Brother and sister definitely looked alike.

"Not sure, buddy," Carter said. "I'm sure your sister is fi—"

That cute face screwed itself into a frown, and a loud cry burst into the air. Carter startled, and the rest of the group laughed with varying degrees of amusement. "And I think that is probably a yes."

"She's got lungs on her, that's for sure," Erin said, shifting the baby in her arms in preparation for handing her over to her husband.

Carter gathered Rayne against his chest. "Wanna help, Thad?"

The boy nodded, and Carter hefted the baby up to his shoulder, walking her off with Thad following.

"While he's here, he can't get enough of being with her," Erin explained. "He sees her when we come home to New York, but I do wish they could be together full-time."

"A blended family is rough," Iris agreed, "but you guys are doing great. And he knows you both love him and that Rayne will too."

"She already does." Erin grinned. "She can't seem to stop smiling and following every move he makes within sight of her when Thad is with her."

Black Wolf's Bluff's postmistress, Lou Rutledge, crowded up behind them, her cats Snookums on a long pink leash. "Erin! Where's that baby?"

Iris took the opportunity to nudge Jamie in the ribs. As they'd spoken, the line behind them had grown, unbeknownst to Iris, and it was definitely time for them to move along. The two of them mingled among the guests for an hour, talking small-town politics, talking horses, talking new books in the library. Iris felt as if the two of them had somehow integrated into Black Wolf's Bluff as a couple without even trying, which had totally surprised her when the realization appeared in her head. No one they ran into asked her about Kirk, no one mentioned him, no one seemed to care that she was recently divorced—a fact that, in a small town like this one, still amazed her. But she was grateful nonetheless.

After they sampled some of Claire's delicious hors d'oeuvres and helped themselves to individual cups of crème brûlée, Jamie took her empty plate and cup and placed them in a nearby receptacle. "What do you say we blow this joint, huh?"

"Oh?" Iris gave him a mischievous side eye. "Want to get some more unpacking done?"

Iris's lease on her apartment, which had been short-term to begin with, had just ended. On a soft summer night only two weeks ago, Jamie had asked her to move in with him. And her heart had melted on the spot. Wake up every morning to this man? Go to sleep cuddled in his arms? It had been one of the easiest decisions of her life despite her lack of desire for marriage. They were committed to each other, both of them knew it, and that was all anyone needed to know.

Would they marry in the future? She didn't know. But they loved each other and were now living together. That was all the commitment she needed.

Jamie groaned, playfully rubbing at his back. "No, not more unpacking."

Iris chuckled. "Well then, did you have something else in mind?"

"I did." Jamie swung to face her, his hands coming up to cup her cheeks. Green eyes darkened as she watched. "Michael's away for the weekend. All the hands are away for the weekend, and I told Marilyn not to come in, in the morning. Which means we have the ranch all to ourselves."

Surprise quickened her heart rate. "What's the special occasion?"

"Your first night at the ranch as my partner in crime."

She pinched his side lightly. "Your 'partner in crime'?"

"Of course!" He leaned in to nuzzle his nose against hers. "You won't let me call you wife yet, so what could be better than to have a partner in crime?"

"Well, I did think you were dangerous the first night we met."

Jamie's grin took on a wicked edge. "Of course I am. To your heart."

To your heart. Truer words were never spoken.

She pulled his face down to hers and lost herself in this man's kiss. When he finally let her up for air, she found herself asking him absentmindedly, "Doesn't everyone being gone mean we have to feed all the horses ourselves?"

Jamie shook his head, then stole another kiss. When someone across the cobblestone yelled, "Get a room, you two"—sounded like JD—he just grinned and followed up with another kiss. "The animals are already taken care of. Everyone was fed before Harris headed out for the night."

Bless that field hand. He was fast becoming Iris's favorite.

"Oh, well in that case..." She hooked her arm through Jamie's. "Let's go say goodbye." They made their way back over to Erin and Carter. Fussy crying could be heard, growing louder as they got closer. Iris felt a whimper rise in her throat in sympathy.

Carter bounced Rayne in his arms, patting her bottom. Erin's hands were full with a plate and cup, her eyes across the courtyard on Thad, who was hurrying over with a folding chair.

The little boy made it within five feet before tripping on the cobblestone and going sprawling. Carter and Erin both released urgent gasps, both reaching for Thad despite full arms.

Carter seemed to come to his senses first. Passing the baby over to Jamie, he tended to Thad while Jamie propped the dark-hair bundle up on his shoulder, where she immediately quieted. Jamie's broad hand sprawled across Rayne's tiny back, and Iris felt herself melt just like she always did around this man.

A whimper escaped her, drawing Jamie's questioning gaze. "What was that?" he asked over the commotion of setting Thad straight and getting Erin settled.

Iris winked. "Just my ovaries exploding," she joked.

Jamie's eyes went dark and hazy, as if he was imagining

exactly what he could do about her response. He proved it when he winked back. "Tell your ovaries to cool their heels and I'll take care of them when we get home."

Iris tipped her head to one side, contemplating the possibilities. "And every other part of me?"

Jamie's grin was downright wicked, the smile she loved, just like she loved him. "You know it, beautiful."

Her smile stretched her face until it ached, a reflection of every happy feeling exploding in her heart. She'd never expected to feel like this after the past year. She'd never expected to find Jamie. But despite the risk, she couldn't be happier that she'd flirted with disaster and come out the other side, knowing who she was, what she deserved, and exactly where to find it.

With Jamie. Always.

～

Did you enjoy *40 AND FLIRTING (WITH DISASTER)*? If so, please consider leaving a review at your favorite retailer to tell other readers about the book. And thank you!

For the latest on the next *SILVER FOXES OF BLACK WOLF'S BLUFF* release (and yes, there will be more!), be sure to sign up for my newsletter here!

About the Author

Born and raised in the Deep South, Ella Sheridan spent years telling herself stories before finally writing her own. Romantic suspense, paranormal romance, sexy contemporaries—she can't seem to stick to just one. Her goal in life is to finish every series she begins (if only she'd stop adding new series so that would be possible!).

Now Ella calls North Alabama home. Spending time cuddling with her two sweet tabbies, Oliver and Henry, is her number one priority, followed closely by writing, working, and writing some more (though she's recently found a little time to learn a new craft: watercolor painting). Connect with Ella at her website or at the social media options below. For news on Ella's new releases, free book opportunities, and more, sign up for Ella's newsletter at ellasheridanauthor.com . Or join Ella's Escape Room on Facebook for daily fun, games, and first dibs on all the news!

www.ingramcontent.com/pod-product-compliance
Lightning Source LLC
Chambersburg PA
CBHW032137170626
46808CB00006B/2269

* 9 7 8 1 9 5 9 5 1 9 2 7 0 *